D0877208

THE COMIC CON

MIDDLE SCHOOL MAYHEM BOOK EIGHT

C.T. WALSH

FARCICAL PRESS

COVER CREDITS

For my Family

Thank you for all of your support

1

There is a place where we nerds can go to escape the outside world. To live within the imaginations of some of the greatest nerds that have ever lived. To avoid peer ridicule, the latest fashion trends, and nerd-destroying activities that our gym teacher claims are character-building sports, like dodgeball. This fabulous place is called Comic Con.

It was the first week of summer after seventh grade and that's where we were headed for the first time. I had begged my father for the past three years to take me, and finally, he agreed. We were packed to the brim in my dad's SUV, third row and all, only miles away from our epic adventure. Little did I know it was going to be epically more epic than I ever imagined and that Comic Con would forever be known to us as *The* Comic Con. We would be witness to a most heinous heist of one of the greatest artifacts (or perhaps I should say fartifacts) ever created. Unbeknownst to us at the time, our lives would be on the line as we attempted to solve the greatest con ever to be committed at Comic Con. But let's not get ahead of ourselves here.

My name is Austin Davenport and, as always, I'm the superhero of this story. Anyone who attempts to convince you otherwise is flat out conning you. My sidekicks with me on this journey are my girlfriend, Sophie, and my friends, Ben, Sammie, Luke, Just Charles, and Cheryl Van Snoogle-Something. If you've been paying attention to any of my previous adventures, you know that I travel with some of the best sidekicks around. One quick warning: keep your arms and legs inside the vehicle at all times and buckle up. It's about to get bumpy.

"The GPS is saying seven minutes, guys!" Luke yelled from the front seat. He was the only one of us without a significant other, so he got to ride up front.

"Okay, some rules for the show," my dad called back to us. "I'll be nearby at my business meeting. I will pick you up at six o'clock as you requested unless you need something. You guys all have your phones. You have money. Call me if you need anything. Stick together and stay out of trouble."

Just a little advanced notice. We did not listen to that last part about trouble. But it was hardly our fault. I'm sure you'll come to agree.

My dad continued, "And Charles, easy on the sugar, dude. The last thing this crazy place needs is Evil Chuck."

Evil Chuck was Just Charles' alter ego that took control when Just Charles' sugar intake was on overload. It was his version of The Hulk, like when Bruce Banner got angry. Evil Chuck wasn't a true villain, just a little reckless. And he could be amusing at times.

Just Charles called up front, "One could argue that this is a safe place for Evil Chuck."

I said, "Those people in there are just pretending while in costume. Evil Chuck is a real villain."

"He's not that bad. Just misunderstood," Just Charles said.

My dad looked into the rear-view mirror and said, "Seriously, I told your mother you would keep it under control."

Sammie asked, "What are we even doing? Who cares about comics anyway?"

If I had been driving, we would've come to a screeching halt, but apparently, my father wasn't bothered by such a ludicrous statement. Sammie and Sophie were the least nerd-like in our group. Sammie was even on the cheerleading squad, so some might understand why she didn't grasp the importance of the hallowed ground we were destined for. I, however, did not understand. I was speechless, which doesn't happen often.

Ben took a deep breath and answered his girlfriend a lot nicer than I would have. "It's not just comic books. There are TV characters, movies, book series, anime. You could see movie stars, famous authors, and meet a ton of cool people just like us."

I regrouped and said, "Dad, we made a huge mistake. Can we drop Sammie off at the next train station?"

Ben said, "Whoa, hey! Let's not get crazy here. Is this how we treat newbies?"

"Okay," I said, looking at Sammie. "You can stay if you answer this question. If you were to get dropped off at any train station in the world, real or fiction, what train station and platform would you choose?"

"Oh, I know! I know!" Just Charles yelled, raising his hand from the back row. "Austin, pick me!"

"It's not for you and no helping."

Sammie thought for a moment. Her future hung in the balance. Everyone in the car held their breath. Finally, Sammie answered, "King's Cross. Platform 9 3/4!"

Everyone in the car cheered at the Harry Potter reference.

"That is correct! You can stay," I said, smiling.

"Gee, thanks," Sammie said.

"I make no apologies. You're on a probationary period right now. I'll check in with you mid-morning and see how you're doing."

"Yes, sir," Sammie said, mockingly.

Sophie smirked, laughing to herself. "You're one of a kind."

"Thanks," I said.

We pulled up to the drop-off section in front of the huge convention center.

"We're here!" I yelled. Excitement surged through my veins. Little did I know the mayhem that was about to ensue would explode past superhero city-endangering mayhem levels.

As we all exited, my dad gave the necessary, but never-listened to advice of, "Don't do anything stupid."

And I gave the typical, lying response with a hint of annoyance, "We won't."

"Have fun."

"Thanks, Dad. This is gonna be awesome."

I closed the car door and slung my backpack over my shoulder. I was gonna need superhero strength just to carry the thing. Between the four boys, we were prepared for anything and everything. Our Comic Con gear consisted of virtually every snack created, maps of the convention center, movie posters, books from our favorite authors, sharpies, and multiple itineraries should we decide to change our minds about where to go.

Sophie looked at me and asked, "Are we planning a military takeover of a small country?"

I smiled and said, "No, but should the opportunity arise, we will be able to manage." Little did I know, there would be multiple wars brewing that we would find ourselves smack dab in the middle of.

2

We hit Comic Con right at the open. Despite that, it was already crowded. And crazy. The convention center was bustling with activity as crowds of people rushed about, trying to hit as many booths as possible before the lines for the panel discussions and other exhibits got too long. Many people were dressed in costumes, ranging from the normal Target and Halloween shop offerings to more elaborate, personally-designed ensembles that rivaled Hollywood costumes.

I looked around, spinning in a circle. "Ahh, my people! I love the smell of comics in the morning!"

"Don't they just smell the same as in the afternoon?" Cheryl Van Snoogle-Something asked.

I shrugged. "Yeah, I guess."

I continued to take in the crazy-awesomeness of it all. If I was the leader of Nerd Nation at Cherry Avenue Middle School, home of the ferocious Gophers, this was Geek Global. I wasn't the General of Geek Global, but perhaps I could work my way up. I would have to start by wearing a costume next time.

"I can't believe we totally ruined the day," Ben said.

"What's the problem?" Sammie asked.

"I knew we should've worn costumes."

"So, buy one," I said, shrugging.

"I don't have enough money to buy a good one and I'm not gonna go weak like that guy in the plastic mask," Ben said, pointing to some dude walking by us in a Black Panther mask.

"Thanks, man," the dude said, sarcastically.

"Sorry, sir," Ben called after him.

"Way to play nice," Luke said, laughing.

"What do we do first?" Sophie asked. "I want to see The Avengers panel and hopefully meet Wonder Woman and go to the children's author and illustrators' panel to see C.T. Walsh."

I looked down at my favorite itinerary. "It's early and we want to hit that panel discussion with C.T. Hopefully, the line won't be too bad getting in. Then we can hit Marvel for The Avengers and then D.C."

Ben chimed in, "We thought we could take turns waiting on the line so we can check stuff out, eat, do whatever, and just save each other's spots."

"Good idea," Just Charles said. "I'm feeling kinda parched. I need to get something to drink."

"I'll go with you," Luke said.

"Okay, Cheryl, you want to go with them and we'll wait on the line?" I asked.

"I'm not sure I really want to be responsible for these two," Cheryl said, laughing. "Is thirty minutes okay?"

"Sure," I said, looking at the map. "It's ballroom C."

"Okay, we'll be back in thirty."

∾

WE FOUND our way to ballroom C and lined up against the wall of a long hallway. I could see the door to the ballroom, but there were probably a hundred people ahead of us in bunches of three or four people. As we waited, we just watched the other people pass by. We saw people dressed as Superman, Spiderman, Thor, Captain America, Batman, Storm Troopers, Wonder Woman, and a host of non-descript elves, princesses, wizards, and a variety of anime characters. It was pretty cool.

The half hour flew by. Cheryl sheperded Luke and Just Charles back to us. Luke was carrying so much stuff that he bought, his backpack was nearly bursting at the seams.

"This place is awesome!" Luke said, with food in his mouth and a half-eaten corn dog on a stick in his hand.

Just Charles sipped on a huge soda that was just under the size of a tub of popcorn.

"Be careful, dude," I said, nodding to his drink. "That's got Evil Chuck written all over it."

Ben added, "Do you really want to go crazy and embarrass yourself in front of all your heroes?"

"It's just one soda. No big deal."

"It's 9:00 A.M." I said.

"Thanks, Mrs. Zaino," Just Charles said, annoyed.

"You call your mother Mrs. Zaino? That's just weird, dude," I said.

"I don't, but I thought it would be weirder to call you Mommy."

"You still call your mother Mommy?" Ben asked.

"No!" Just Charles said, defensively.

"What's going on out there?" Ben asked, as if he hadn't seen it for the last thirty years, let alone thirty minutes.

"There are some wackos out there," Cheryl said.

"But some really cool costumes," Just Charles added.

"And merch. The merch is amazing," Luke said, patting his backpack.

"Where do you want to go?" Sophie looked at me and asked.

"I want to check out all those little tables and stands with memorabilia and stuff. But let's wait a little while. I want the people around us to know there's seven of us, so they don't think we're line cutters. I hate that."

"Good idea."

"What's this panel about?" Cheryl asked.

Ben said, "I was reading online that C.T. is gonna announce an eight-book superhero series, ready for pre-order tonight. He's going to launch all of them at the same time in about a month."

"Is that true?" Luke asked.

"Don't know, but people are pumped. His panel should be packed. He's supposed to talk about it today."

"Where did you read that?" Just Charles asked, after taking a huge slurp of his vat of soda.

"I read it on a blog that follows C.T.'s career. It's called Fartstorm.com or was it fartsinfiction.com?"

"How many fart blogs do you read?" Sammie asked, concerned.

"All of them," Ben said, proudly.

Some lady who was standing in front of us turned around and chimed in, "C.T. is so amazing. And handsome." She looked to the girls for confirmation.

Sammie shrugged.

The woman had a huge wig and makeup caked on like she had been in a bakery explosion. I had no idea what costume she was wearing and wasn't about to ask.

"Oh, I hope I meet him," she said, gushing. "He's so fartastic."

"Did you say fartastic?" Sophie asked.

"Yes. I made it up to describe him."

"This place is weirder than I thought," I whispered to Ben.

And then some dude dressed in a cape cut into the line right ahead of us, ignoring us.

"What's that all about?" Sammie asked.

"Excuse me, sir. There's a line. It starts around the corner," I said.

"We've been waiting," Sophie added.

The man turned his head and said over his shoulder, "Good for you. Keep waiting."

"What?" Sophie asked, annoyed.

"Is there a problem?" the man asked, turning around fully, his cape fanning out behind him. It was a bit more dramatic than necessary.

"I guess it's fine," I said, putting my hand on Sophie's

shoulder. She was not yet ready to attack, but I could sense she was thinking about it.

"You guess?" the man asked, pointedly.

"It's fine," I said.

"Rudeness," Sophie added.

The man turned around again, this time more aggressively. He got caught in his cape and shook his arms out of it, annoyance growing with each thrust. Finally, he was free of his cape and turned his nose back up at us. "If you must know, I was here, but I had to go to the restroom. Not that it's any of your business."

"Was it number one or number two?" I asked, to laugher from my crew.

"What's it to you?"

"I want to see if you're telling the truth."

"I don't have to tell you anything."

"That's what somebody who cuts kids and lies about it says." I looked over at Ben and whispered enough so the grumpy man could hear, "Maybe it was 1 1/2 and he's too embarrassed to answer."

"Kids!" the man said, turning his back on us. I dodged his cape with the speed of Barry Allen, The Flash.

"Yeah, the problem is us," Sophie responded. "Says the man wearing tights and a cape."

"That was fun," Sammie said, unenthused.

"Anyway," I said. "I wonder what the panel is gonna be like. I guess there will be a moderator." I paused for a moment and then fear bubbled up inside of me. "Oh, no! What if it's Calvin?" Calvin Conklin was our local newscaster, who seemed to ruin every event he attended, most recently the Cupid's Cutest Couple Contest Sophie and I had entered together.

"Oh, God. Please no," Sophie said.

"No, he's not the local news man here," Cheryl said. "We're too far from home."

"Oh, good," I said.

Ben said, "This guidebook says there's a comic book artist from Marvel on the panel. Some other fart-joke author, Jimmy O'Beans."

Luke said, "that sounds fartastic," but not really paying attention. His eyes were fixated on a tween Wonder Woman headed our way, walking with what looked like her older sister in a Black Widow costume from Avengers.

"Whoa, hey there," Luke said.

Wonder Woman smiled at Luke as she walked by. They joined a few people on line a few steps back.

"That is some woman," Luke said, craning his neck to see her.

"She's wonderful," Cheryl said. "You know, there's more to her than how she looks." She elbowed Just Charles.

"She's right," Just Charles said.

"Can you take a picture of the guys?" I asked Sophie.

"Sure."

We lined up shoulder to shoulder and smiled. And then I got punched in the face by Ben as he pointed past me toward Thor, the God of Thunder. I was totally okay with it.

"Thor!" we all yelled, giddy.

"This is unreal!" Just Charles yelled.

"You know he's not real, right? It's just a dude in a costume." Sammie said, unimpressed. Her probationary period was not working out all that well.

"Hey, Thor!" I yelled. "Can you join us for a picture?" I crossed my fingers.

The man dressed as Thor stopped and smiled. "Of course!" he bellowed. "It's always a pleasure to meet the citizens and future leaders of Asgard." Thor towered over us and he stood behind me and stretched his arms from Ben's shoulders on the end to my left and Luke's shoulders on the end to my right.

"Did you hear that?" I whispered to Sophie, as she steadied her iPhone. "Future leader of Asgard?"

"Yes. It's very impressive," she said, less than impressed.

Sophie snapped the picture as I smiled from ear to ear.

"Looks good," Sophie said.

"Do a bunch more, rapid fire," I said.

"Okay," Sophie said, firing away.

I turned around and fist bumped Thor. "Thank you."

"It's my pleasure," Thor said, flipping his cape off his shoulder.

His cape flew out into the walkway behind him and hit a woman rolling by in a wheel chair.

"Hey, watch it, you Nordic Neanderthal," she said, rudely.

"C.T. Walsh is coming," a voice called out.

Others yelled, "C.T.! Can I have an autograph?"

A lady fainted behind us, as the crowd chatter rose.

Another person yelled at C.T. "How could you kill off Gemini?"

"Oh, my goodness. He's a dreamboat!" the crazy woman yelled, as she thrust herself toward C.T., her arms outstretched for a hug. "I just want a quick hug and a kiss!"

The woman smacked Thor in the face, as she jumped on the Shakespeare of Fart Jokes, also known as C.T. Walsh. She wrapped her arms around him while he tried to extract himself.

"Oww," Thor whined, as he stumbled back. Thor reached out and grabbed my shirt and Ben's as well. The force of the Norse God was too much for nerds like us to handle. We all crashed into the woman in the wheelchair behind him. I looked up to see Luke's corn dog soaring through the air.

C.T. dove for it, yelling, "Not on my watch!" He hurdled over a bag on the ground and stretched his hand out, the corn dog spraying mustard every which way as it spiraled toward the ground. C.T's voice seemed to shift to slow motion, "Eeeeye gaaaaaaht ihhhht!" The level of intensity was off-the-charts insane, as we watched the fiction phenom float through the air.

The crazy woman was air born right behind C.T. We all landed in a crunch with some yelps and mustard splatter.

We were a jumbled heap of arms, legs, Thor's hammer, a wheelchair, and a corn dog without much mustard. Before I knew what was happening, the woman from the wheelchair was on top of Thor, whacking him with his own hammer. Repeatedly. He held his forearms and hands in front of his face and head, shielding himself from the vicious attack. It hurt just as much for me as it did for him, as I had to fully accept that it was not the real Thor. It was truly just a man in a suit. True, I was not going to have the physical bruises to match, but trust me, it was painful.

I lay on my back as we all attempted to get up at the same time, which proved to be a mistake. The continuous jostling just kept us down. We nerds find it tough to coordinate ourselves. Coordinate with a whole group? It was a comedy show. And then darkness fell upon me as a cape slapped me in the face. I fumbled with it. Eventually, I crumpled the cape into a ball and threw it to the side. I looked over to see it was attached to the grumpy man. A hand reached out to me. I grabbed it, not paying attention to who it was coming from. When I got to my feet, I realized that C.T. was standing in front of me, having just helped me up. He held the corn dog in his hand, a huge smile across his face.

"Did you see that catch I made? That was legit, if I do say so myself," C.T. said, smiling.

"Umm, yeah. It was pretty good," I said, not believing that I was talking to my favorite author about diving corn-dog catches.

"Sorry about the mustard," he said, pointing to the splatter on my shirt. "But in fairness, it's not even my corn dog." C.T. took a bite of it anyway.

"That's okay," I said.

"It looks spicy," he said, adjusting his bag over his shoulder. "There's no mustard left on this one."

"Why does that matter?"

He shrugged. "Spicy mustard is more exciting."

"Are you okay?" Sophie asked, after having made her way through the commotion. I was thinking of asking C.T. the same question.

But C.T. beat me to it. "That's a good question," C.T. said. He called out to the rest of the group, "Everybody okay?"

I noticed a trail of blood on the floor.

C.T. must've noticed it, too. He looked at the woman comfortably back in her wheelchair and pointed to the cut on her hand. "Do you need anything for that? Are you okay?"

"Yeah, you stupid buffoon!" The woman thrust her fist forward lightning quick, like it was powered by the Thunder God himself.

C.T. doubled over in pain. He took a deep breath and

stood back up. "Not sure I deserved that, but thankfully, my abs of steel absorbed most of the massive blow," C.T. said through gritted teeth, while holding his stomach. He looked at the woman and narrowed his eyes. I thought he was going to say something revengeful, but instead asked, "Did you fart?"

"No, I think it was Thor."

"He *is* the God of Thunder," C.T. said, shrugging.

He looked back at Sophie and me. "That took a lot out of me. I was at least eight inches off the ground, diving for that dog. Do you think that's some sort of record?" He took another bite. "This is tasty. This place is the best. There are literally corn dogs falling from the sky. Have you ever been anywhere that has delicious food falling from the sky? I mean, Cloudy With a Chance of Meatballs wasn't real. It was just a movie. This is a real-life corn dog."

"I can't say that I have," I said. It was all kind-of weird, but before I could say more, another commotion broke out. There were people jostling around and a woman yelled, "Get your hands off me!"

"What's going on?" I asked, craning my neck over the crowd.

A short, burly security guard was locked onto the arm of the lady that had tried to hug and kiss C.T.

"Let's go, lady. You're outta here," the security guard said.

C.T. interjected, "Officer, this was nobody's fault. No need for anyone to get into trouble, except whoever was hitting me with Thor's hammer."

Thor stared down at the floor, no hammer in sight. The security guard ignored C.T. and pushed the woman through the crowd.

"What's that all about? How did he even know what she

did?" C.T. said, rushing after them. But they disappeared into the crowd before he could catch them.

A minute later, he was back. "I think I had a water bottle. Anybody see my water bottle?"

He didn't realize it at the time- none of us did- but something much more important had gone missing. His soul... Just kidding. But still, it was big.

I was still smarting from physical injuries from the collision and the emotional trauma of having another dude's cape in my face. It might not sound like a big deal, but in the superhero world, there are few things more embarrassing. One of them is getting beaten with your own hammer, by the way.

I rubbed my elbow as the crowd thinned. C.T. looked back in my direction and looked down at my elbow.

"Was that your elbow that shattered my spleen? Spleen. Spleens are so silly. Spleen, spleen, spleen, spleen, spleen," C.T. said, seemingly pleased with himself or at least amusing himself.

"Sorry about that," I said. "That was quite the kerfuffle."

"What a great word. And don't worry about it. I'm not even sure what my spleen does. Can't be that important." C.T. gripped his side with a wince and a groan.

Sophie jumped forward. "Are you okay?"

C.T. stood up. "Just kidding. Spleen jokes never get old."

"That's the first one I've ever heard," I said.

C.T. wiped a fake tear from his eye. "That's one of the saddest things I've ever heard. By the way, your elbows are pretty bony. You should get that checked out."

And then Cheryl said, "Ewww, what's that smell?"

I was pretty sure C.T. farted. Or somebody stepped on a duck. But then he looked at me and said, "Dude, I can't believe you just farted."

"It wasn't me," I said, defensively.

"You sure?" he asked, and then shrugged. "This area is known to have a large population of Barking Tree Frogs."

"I'll keep an eye out for them," I said, not sure how serious he was.

"Be sure that you do. They're very dangerous."

Sophie looked at C.T.'s bag over his shoulder and said, "Your...purse is ripped."

C.T. took a step back. "Excuse me?" he asked, shocked. "It's a man bag."

"But it's not manly," Sammie chimed in.

C.T. said, "There is no true reality. There is only perception."

"What does that mean?" I asked.

"I don't know, but we're not talking about my man bag anymore, are we?"

"Yes, we are," I said.

"Dang it," C.T. said, annoyed. "You're good. But look, under there." C.T. pointed behind me.

"Under where?" I asked, turning.

"Ha ha. I made you say underwear."

"That's lame," Sophie said.

"Perhaps, but we're not talking about my man bag anymore, are we?"

"We are!" I said.

"Double dang it. You know what? I'm not ashamed to use a man bag. I mean look at this fine, hand crafted-" C.T. paused as he stared at the bag, and then continued, "piece of garbage." The bag was ripped down the side of it. "Wait a second." CT looked at the bag more closely. "What the heck?"

"What's wrong?" I asked. "Besides your man bag being torn to shreds beyond repair."

C.T. opened the bag and looked inside. "It feels kinda light. Oh, no. My laptop is missing! Oh, God. This is terrible." C.T. looked up at the ceiling, took a deep breath, and then looked back at us. "My new series is in there."

"It's backed up, right?" I asked.

"Yeah, but that's not the problem," he said, pacing. "Piracy is the problem."

We stood with C.T., trying to figure out what it all meant.

"Pirates!" Luke yelled.

CHAPTER 4

We stood around C.T., not sure what to do. Luke looked at Just Charles and said, "Pirates, dude. Things just got awesome." Luke looked at C.T. and said, "Oh, sorry."

C.T. said, "Not those kind of pirates. Digital pirates."

"Still, that sounds pretty cool," Luke said. "Do they have swords?"

"Yes, of the finest steel," C.T. said, mockingly. The problem is, guys, somebody could just release it to the world and everything I worked for goes up in smoke. All the money it could've made will be gone. I was gonna use that money to start a school for underprivileged kids. And it took me two years to write that series."

"Is it password protected?" Just Charles asked.

"Yes. It's farts1234. Is that secure?"

"No," Ben said.

"I'm joking. That's not the password, but this is bad."

And then my eye caught something up against the wall. It wasn't good. "The bag didn't just rip. It was cut." I pointed to the box cutter, pressed up against the molding.

"This is so bad," C.T. said.

"What's going on here?" a male voice boomed.

We looked up to see a security guard assessing the scene. He was bald with a goatee. The buttons on his shirt threatened to pop off at any moment.

"Everybody, step to the side here."

C.T. rushed over to him. "Sir, someone stole my computer." He lifted his bag to show the security guard the torn man bag.

The guard pressed the button on the walkie-talkie attached to his shoulder and spoke into it, "We've got a code four-niner in progress."

Thor rushed over to him as well. "She hit me...with my own hammer," he said, pointing to the woman in the wheelchair.

The guard frowned. "We've also got a code chartreuse."

C.T. looked at Thor and said, "My code is so much cooler than yours. I got a four-niner, man."

Thor frowned. "Why do I get a code chartreuse?"

The guard looked unimpressed. "You got beat up by a girl."

"They have a code for that?" C.T. asked.

"They have a code for everything. Plus, dudes get beat up by girls all the time at Comic Con. This place is a nerd fest."

Thor slumped his shoulders and walked away.

The guard pulled out a pad from his fanny pack.

"Nice pack, man. I need more space, so that's why I got this man bag, but I like how you roll," C.T. said with a thumbs up.

"Yeah, thanks," the guard said, sarcastically.

The guard readied his pen on the pad. "What's your name?"

"C.T. Walsh."

"Who else was involved?"

"There were so many people on the line and in the pile-up, even. I don't know."

"Everybody still here?"

"No, but I don't know who's missing. The lady who kept trying to kiss me is gone."

I walked over and added, "And the grumpy dude."

"Yeah, the grumpy dude," C.T. said. "Who was that?" he asked me.

"The dude in the tights and the cape," I said.

"You'll have to be more specific. Half the dudes in here are dressed like that," the guard said.

"He was grumpy," I said, unhelpfully. I really hoped it was him. I wanted to see him behind bars. Yeah, it may be a little dark, but line-cutting is a serious offense, especially when it's a kid without a parent. No, I'm not an orphan, but he didn't know that. He very well could've been cutting an orphan. The man was a menace and needed to be stopped.

"Anyone else?"

"C.T. pointed to the lady in the wheel chair and Thor. They were involved. And she punched me in the stomach. I don't need a code chartreuse. I'm just warning you. Keep your distance."

The guard continued to pepper C.T. with questions. I turned back to my friends.

"This is awesome," Ben said. "Well, besides the crime that could ruin C.T.'s career."

My eyes bulged as the tween Wonder Woman returned and stood behind Luke. She was lurking, just like he did. We called him, Luke the Lurker. He was always surprising us.

"What's going on?" she asked.

Luke jumped and then turned around. He stared at her for a moment.

"Hi," Wonder Woman said. "I'm Diana."

"Luke," he said, cooly.

"Like from Star Wars?"

"Yeah, totally."

"Where's your costume?"

"I, umm, gave it to some needy kid."

"Oh, how sweet."

I said to Wonder Woman, "Maybe you should hit some of these people with the lasso of truth. We'll solve the case in no time."

"It's not real."

"They don't have to know," Ben said.

"I'm not doing that," she said.

"That's less than wonderful," I said. "When did you lose the wonder?"

"Don't be rude to our new friend," Luke said, staring me down.

Just Charles stepped forward and took the lasso from Wonder Woman's belt. "Here, let me see that." Just Charles inspected it for a moment and then snapped it out.

The whip cracked, smacking C.T. in the butt. He jumped and yelped, as he spoke to the security guard.

"Why'd you do that?" C.T. asked, angrily. C.T. took the whip out of Just Charles' hand. "This thing is kind of awesome." His face morphed into a smile as he inspected it.

"Be careful with it," the security guard said. "The medical center is already filled with weaponry injuries. And code chartreuses," he said, staring at Thor.

"Don't worry, man. I watched all the Indiana Jones movies and Wonder Woman. I know how to handle a whip." C.T. cracked the whip out to his side.

The whip smacked Thor in the butt. He shrieked like a kindergartener and fell to his knees.

C.T. handed the whip back to Wonder Woman, a sheepish look on his face. "It just went off on its own. Be careful with that."

"I'm gonna talk to some of these people," the security guard said. "The police are on the way. Just wait here for a few minutes."

"Thank you," C.T. said. He turned around, walked toward us, and pulled out his phone. He dialed and held it to his ear. "Kyle, where are you? Okay. Big problem. My laptop was stolen...Yeah, I know...I'm waiting for the police. Anyway, you can remote into the laptop and remove the book files? Yeah, I didn't think so. Thought I would try. There's a password, but they cut into my man bag and took it. I think it was premeditated...Yeah, okay. I'll see you over there." C.T. hung up the phone. He looked at us accusingly and said, "So, which one of you stole my laptop?"

We all looked around at each other, stuttering.

C.T. laughed. "Just kidding. Thank you for your help."

"No problem," I said. I introduced myself and all of my friends.

"It's nice to meet you all. I'm C.T."

"We know. We're big fans," I said.

"Oh, well, thank you." C.T. looked down at the empty corn dog stick in his hand. He turned around and saw a garbage pail against the wall. He looked back at us and tossed the stick over his shoulder. "Incoming!" he yelled.

The stick tumbled end over end, heading toward the garbage pail. It was on target for a direct hit. That is, until Thor walked in front of it. The stick hit Thor in the side of the head and fell to the ground.

"Owww!" Thor yelled, his hand pulled to his face like a magnet.

C.T. turned around and then returned quickly to us.

"Oops. So, I need to take my mind off all of this. Ask me anything."

"Did you really fart over there?" I asked.

"Wow. This is a tough crowd. But good question. Who's got another one?"

Sophie said, "Tell us about your next series."

"It's called The Farthing Chronicles."

"What's it about?" Ben asked.

"It's highly classified, but I'll tell you about the main character. Her name is Ima. Ima Farthing." He stared at us. "I'm kidding. That's not it at all. It's about super heroes."

"What kind of super powers do the characters have?" Sophie asked.

"The main character has a super colon."

"You spent two years writing about a super hero who has supersonic farts?" Just Charles asked.

"Yeah, do you think I wasted my time?" C.T. asked, concerned.

"No! That sounds awesome!" Ben yelled.

The girls shook their heads with pity.

C.T.'s phone rang. He answered it. "Hey, Kyle. Nothing yet...There's not much we can do...unless we try to solve the mystery ourselves...Oh, okay. I'll see you in a few." He hung up the phone and looked at us. "Sorry, guys. Let's do this again sometime, but I really need to find my laptop." He waved and headed back to the security guard.

"So, what do we got?" I asked my crew.

"Umm, we have Pirates Booty, pretzels, cookies..." Ben said, his voice trailing off.

"No, I meant with the case. C.T. talked about solving the crime ourselves."

"He wasn't serious," Sammie said.

"So? Why can't we try to solve it?" I asked.

"I'm in," Cheryl said, enthusiastically and not surprisingly. She was an investigative journalist for our school newspaper, The Gopher Gazette, so moving to detective work wasn't that much of a stretch. Her skills had saved me a few times.

"It beats waiting," Sophie said.

"Plus, think about how cool it will be to solve a real case. For C.T. Walsh!" Ben said.

"Who could it be?" I asked. "My money's on the grumpy guy."

"What about that angry guy? Some dude was yelling at him about Gemini," Sophie said.

I looked around. "Neither of those guys are still here, which is weird, because the grumpy guy was on line for the panel."

"Maybe he cut some poor orphan kid closer to the front," I said.

"Huh?" Sammie said.

"Long story."

"What costume was grumpy guy in?" Cheryl asked.

"Don't know," Just Charles said. "I don't think it was a character."

"Yeah, he was just a random dude in tights and a cape," Luke said.

"That's disturbing," Sophie said.

"Totally," I said. "I never go out in public with mine."

Two police officers arrived and started talking to the security guard. After a few minutes, they separated and began taking statements from everyone.

One of the police officers, Sergeant Villone, addressed the crowd. He adjusted his hat and glasses and said, "Excuse me, folks! If you witnessed the crime, I'd ask you to stay in the area until we take your statement."

"We're not going anywhere," somebody said, monotone.

"Now, where is the victim?" the other officer, Patrolman Yasmanian asked.

I stepped forward. "He's not here at the moment. He was called away."

"Called away? What does that mean?"

"Someone called and he went away," I said.

"Were you here for the criminal act?" Sergeant Villone said, pulling down his glasses and staring down his nose at me.

"Umm, yes. But I didn't know a crime had taken place until well after the pile up."

"Pile up?" Sergeant Villone asked.

"Is everyone still here that was involved in this pile up?" Officer Yasmanian asked.

"No. There was some lady who tried to kiss C.T. A security guard left with her. There was a grumpy dude. You might want to look into him. There was also another dude yelling at C.T. I don't know who else left. The rest of us," I said, pointing to my crew, "are still here. That lady over there and Thor were also involved. And there's probably an assault that needs to be reported, but I'll leave that to Thor."

"Who is this C.T. guy?"

"He's an author. It was his laptop that was stolen."

The police officer was writing down my every word. It was kinda cool. If it wasn't so serious, I would start saying stupid stuff, just to see if he would write it down.

"And can you describe the grumpy guy you mentioned?"

"Definitely. He was very grumpy. He cut me on the line. You should probably investigate that. Some of these kids could be orphans. Most of them probably are."

"Yeah, we'll add it to the list, kid. That's right after we figure out which Hulk clogged the toilet."

"Gross," Sophie said. "They report that to the police?"

"Yeah. It was that bad."

"Was it green?" I asked.

"No comment." Sergeant Villone looked at me. "I need a physical description."

"Right. Black hair. He wore tights and a cape. It was black."

"This is great stuff," the officer said, writing it down. "Anything else? Did he have a face you could describe?"

"He did have a face," I said, thinking aloud.

"He had a scruffy beard, green eyes, and his teeth were crooked and a touch yellow," Sophie said.

"Yeah, all that stuff," I said. I looked at Sophie and said, "How did you remember all that stuff?"

The officer finished writing.

"Oh, my God!" Sophie yelled, excitedly. "I've got it! The pictures!" She pulled out her phone and pulled up her photo app.

I leaned over and checked out the pictures on her phone, as she flipped through them. "Oh, that's a good one," I said, looking at a picture of my nostril. "Oooh, is that Thor's nose hair?"

"Knock it off," Sophie said. "There has to be a good one in here."

Sergeant Villone shook his head. "Don't go anywhere."

"Can we help with the investigation?" I asked the officer.

"Yeah. You can help by going and getting a picture with Iron Man."

While I wasn't a huge fan of Tony Stark's ego, I was impressed with his science and technology talents. "How is that gonna help?"

"It's gonna keep you outta my hair," the officer said.

"This isn't a joke, kid. Leave this to the professionals." Sergeant Villone walked away and over to Thor.

I shook my head and watched Sophie go through the pictures. "There's C.T.'s man bag."

"And here's C.T.," C.T. said, seemingly appearing out of nowhere. "You solve the case yet?"

"Not yet," I said.

"There's the lady's wig," C.T. said, pointing to a picture. "That's a sweet action shot, Sophie. Look at how that curl is in mid bounce. You've got a good eye for photography."

"Thanks," Sophie said, smiling.

"Don't show him the one of my nose hair," I said.

"No, I would love to see that," C.T. said, excitedly.

"You would?" I asked, concerned.

"No. Absolutely not. Erase those immediately."

We all laughed.

"There was something about that lady. She just wasn't real."

"She was wearing a wig," Ben said.

"It was more than that. She was just so over the top. It was like fake or something."

"What are you trying to say? I'm ugly? She didn't really want to kiss me?" C.T. asked, agitated.

"No," I said, apologetically.

"I'm just kidding. You're right. Nobody is that crazy about anyone, regardless of how handsome he is. Or how fabulous his fart jokes are," C.T. said. "There's more to me than just looks."

"But you are very fashionable," Sophie quipped.

"Looks like I'm not the only one who knows how to wield the sword of sarcasm. Maybe we should co-author something together."

Cheryl chimed in, "She's going to be running for class president. We can't have her associated with fart jokes."

"That's fair enough."

Sergeant Villone finished up his interview of a nearby witness. C.T. caught his eye and said, "Excuse me, Officer? I'm C.T. Walsh. It was my laptop that was stolen."

"Oh, okay, sir. I'll take your statement." The officer flipped to a new page in his note pad.

C.T. looked around and asked, "Are there security tapes?"

"We'll have to check them and see what we can find. It's so crowded and there are so many people with capes, wigs, and masks, I'm not sure it's gonna show anything," Officer Yasmanian answered.

"So, you want to tell me what happened?" Sergeant Villone looked at C.T. expectantly.

"There's not much to say. There was a big kerfuffle." C.T. gave me a thumbs up. "Some dude was yelling at me. The lady who disappeared was trying to kiss me before she disappeared. Thor was farting on everybody. And I'm sure you heard about the grumpy dude. There was an errant corn dog and even a Barking Tree Frog. I also got punched in the gut by some lady. I'm still not sure why. Maybe it was her corn dog? Once I started thinking about it, I realized it probably didn't really fall from the sky."

"Corn dogs falling from the sky? A barking what? Thor farting?" Sergeant Villone asked, and then took a deep breath. "Every year, I say I'm taking a vacation day during Comic Con but every year, I always work Comic Con."

"Tell me about the disappearing woman," Officer Yasmanian said.

"She was trying to kiss me. I don't know why security took her away. It wasn't that big of a deal."

"Well, you are a very handsome man," the sergeant said, cleaning his glasses.

"I'm going to enjoy that before you put your clean glasses back on."

"What do you mean?" Sergeant Villone asked, putting his glasses back on. "Oh, yeah. You're right. These things do work."

"Glad I could be of service."

"What's on the laptop?"

"Usual stuff. Blackmail on my enemies. Sinister plans. My unpublished book series."

"Come again?"

"Just kidding," C.T. said, with a smile. "Well, not about the unpublished book series. I'm afraid it could be pirated."

"Pirates are cool. I would love to catch a pirate." He looked up at C.T. after realizing what he had said, and then, in an official voice, continued, "Do you have a strong password?"

"It's farts1234. Is that good? Seriously, I have a biometric fingerprint scanner. So that should be good security. They'll have a real hard time cracking that. We'll find them before then."

I interrupted. "Did you find your water bottle yet?"

"No," C.T. said. He looked at the officer. "My water bottle is missing. Do you think they could use that to lift my fingerprint?"

"Anything is possible."

"Look, I really need to get the laptop back and stop whoever did this."

"We're doing our best. We'll look into it. Anything else you want to add to the statement?"

"Not really."

"Well, good luck. We'll be in touch if we make any progress."

"Thank you, Officer."

C.T. turned around, a frown on his face. "They're never gonna solve this."

"We can help," I said. "We're in."

"Team high five?" C.T. asked.

I stared at his outstretched hand. Nobody on my crew moved.

"Why are you so afraid of a high five?"

"Hashtag: nerd problems," Just Charles said.

"Dude, don't talk in hashtags," Luke said.

"Yeah, that's hashtag: not cool," C.T. said. He looked at his watch and said, "I gotta go again, guys. My meeting was postponed. It's starting in a few minutes."

"We gotta wait on the line. We can't really help that much."

"Waiting for my session?"

"Yep," I said.

"Don't worry about that. I have a bunch of seats blocked off in the front. How many are you? Seven? I can accommodate that. Just talk to my assistant, Kyle. He'll be off to the side of the stage, looking official. Sound good?"

We all nodded, smiling.

C.T. continued, "You just have to cheer really loud for me. More than you do for the other dudes. Especially, Jimmy O'Beans. Got it?"

"Yep. We'll boo Jimmy," Ben said.

"Even better," C.T. said, smiling.

After C.T. walked away, we decided to walk around and brainstorm, since we didn't need to wait on line anymore.

"So, the crazy lady," She said. "She wasn't carrying anything, but a small purse."

"It was smaller than C.T.'s man bag," Sammie said.

"How do you even know this stuff?" I asked.

They ignored me. Cheryl said, "So, she couldn't have taken it."

"What about under her dress?" Just Charles asked.

"How would she have done that?" Ben asked.

I chimed in, "I don't know, but Thor's hammer almost went up my butt, so I guess anything is possible."

We stopped in front of a Star Wars light saber stand. The boys and I totally stopped paying attention to any talk of purses, despite the fact that we were trying to solve C.T.'s laptop mystery.

"I'm totally getting one of these," I said, picking one up.

A nerdy shop keeper tossed a Yoda mask aside and walked over to us. "Do you feel the force in that one?"

"Depends on how much it costs," I said.

"Ninety-nine Imperial credits, usually, but I can sell it to you for seventy-nine."

"Yeah, I'm not sensing much forcical connection with this one after all," I said, putting it back.

After we walked past a few Storm Troopers who appeared to inspect us carefully, Luke said, "What about C.T.'s assistant?"

"Kyle?" I asked.

"He wasn't even there," Ben said.

"That we know of," I countered.

Sophie said, "He could've been in costume."

"I think it's called a disguise when you're doing something dubious," Just Charles said.

"Thanks," Sophie said, with a smirk.

"I can't wait to see how big his butt is," Luke said.

"Huh?" Sophie asked.

"He could've hidden it in his butt."

"Maybe we should look at his face first and see if he was actually there before we check out his butt," I suggested.

"Good idea."

"Thor was wearing a fake beard. Maybe it was him," Sammie offered.

"C.T. would've known his voice, though, right?"

"Right," I said, disappointed. "Either way, we have to move fast. They can release this thing in no time. If they can hack the password, it can go right away."

Cheryl chimed in, "Do you think they could've taken his water bottle to steal his finger prints?"

I nodded. "I think it's likely. This is bad," I said, copying C.T. Ahhh, farts was probably more appropriate, but whatever.

CHAPTER 5

We didn't know what to do. The crowds around us grew. Everyone was trying to figure out what had happened. The police taped off a section of the hallway that caused a huge amount of chaos, as the scene of the crime was a high-traffic hallway. A few dudes dressed as Superman tried to fly over the tape, but none were successful. They just kept tearing it down. The Invisible Man might have been successful, but I guess we'll never know. Eventually, they just left the tape down and the hallway was back open. We got as close to the scene as we could, just observing the police and trying to listen for clues.

After about ten minutes, Just Charles yelled, "Snack break!"

"What the-" Sophie said, frowning at me. "From what? We're just sitting around."

"Sorry. You can't ignore a snack break. It's man code going back thousands of years."

"That's ridiculous," Sammie said.

"So is going to the bathroom with a buddy, but you don't see us trying to stop it."

Dozens of dudes, dressed in all kinds of costumes, followed suit, pulling out granola bars, beef jerky, and candy bars. A guy dressed as Zorro even broke out chips, salsa, and guacamole.

We found an empty table in the food court. It was still early enough that people weren't looking for lunch yet.

"What clues do we have?" Cheryl asked.

"Well, we have the awesome photos," I said.

Sophie shot her eye lasers at me. "That's not my fault. I didn't know it was going to be the scene of the crime or that your nostrils would attack my camera lens."

"I didn't have any boogies, did I?"

"Ewww," Sophie said.

"So, we got nothin'" Ben said.

"Well, security and the police are searching the scene. They won't let us anywhere near it," Just Charles said.

"Why don't we check out the escape route? We never followed that blood trail," I said, a little excited. Not that I was happy about people bleeding everywhere, but we had a trail to follow.

"Should we split up? We need to find the grumpy dude," Ben said.

"My dad said not to," I said.

"It's only down each hallway," Luke said. "I don't need you to protect me."

"Let's send out a search party for all the suspects," Cheryl said. "Thor, Grumpy Dude, Crazy Lady. And we've got the other suspect right here."

"I'm not a suspect," I said.

"You're my suspect then," Cheryl said.

"You're not even a detective."

Cheryl faked sadness. "That hurts."

CHAPTER 6

Our crew split up. Ben, Sammie, Sophie, and I stuck together, while the others went in the opposite direction, searching for clues, and stopping for snacks on the way, no doubt. We discussed the case and potential clues, as we looked for suspects and headed back toward the scene of the crime to follow the blood trail.

"What happened to the grumpy dude?" Sophie asked.

"He had a backpack stuffed with snacks," I said.

Sophie and Sammie looked at me like that was somehow totally useless information.

I shrugged. "I was hungry. The Pirates' Booty looked good. I guess he could've hidden a laptop there."

"And why did he disappear?" Sophie asked.

I nodded my head. "He's totally guilty."

"Based on what?" Ben asked.

"He already flouted the line cutting rules. He's a floutist!" I yelled.

"Isn't Buthaire always calling you that?" Sammie asked.

"I'm a flouterer," I said. "There's a difference."

"No, there isn't," Sammie said, doubtfully.

"There is. A flouterer flouts rules that are supposed to be broken, while a floutist is just a jerk, breaking rules," I said. "Look it up."

"Let's get the heck out of here," Ben said.

"What's going on?" Sammie asked.

Ben nodded across the hallway. "It looks like The Joker and Spiderman are about to get into it."

"That's not The Joker. He's dressed like a hobo."

"He's not a hobo," Ben said.

"What? Hobos can't have a beef with Spiderman?"

"That girl is dressed like Harley Quinn. She's The Joker's girlfriend."

"Maybe," I said, not willing to admit my mistake.

"Let's head down this way," Ben said, waving us away from the growing commotion.

"People really are getting into character," Sophie said. "It's a little bit surreal."

As we walked down the corridor, I asked, "What's the motive? Just a random thief trying to get a laptop?"

"Who's to say the criminal knew what was in the purse?" Sophie asked.

"Man bag," I corrected.

"You're right. Not about the purse, but the thief might not even have known C.T. or what was in the purse," Sophie said.

"Well, the dude who cut us knew who he was and the lady did, too," I said.

"Did Thor? How about the lady in the wheelchair?" Ben asked.

Ben said, "She wasn't waiting on the line. She was just passing through, I think. The same with Thor."

"Do you think the Viking God of Thunder knows who C.T. Walsh is?" I asked.

"Thor doesn't strike me as much of a reader," Sammie said.

"I'm pretty certain Thor likes fart jokes, though," I said.

Sammie put her hands on her hips. "How are you pretty certain?"

"Guys. We've got bigger issues," Sophie said. "Is this what you argue about when girls aren't around?"

"Pretty much."

Ben said, "Batman totally likes fart jokes."

I rolled my eyes. "No way. He hates farts in general. You can't have a suit like his and like farts or fart jokes."

"Guys!" Sophie yelled.

"Oh, right," I said. 'Sorry."

"So, I hate to say this," Sophie said. "If half the people didn't know who C.T. was- and even if they did, it's unlikely that they would know his laptop would be in his bag or what would be on his laptop, right?"

"Right," Ben said.

"Where are you going with this?" Sammie asked.

"Is it out of the question that he could've orchestrated this himself?" Sophie said, biting her lip.

"Preposterous!" I yelled.

"Is it?" Sophie asked.

Ben shook his head. "Why would he do that?"

Sophie tapped her chin as she spoke. "I don't know. To generate publicity? Maybe get on the news. I mean, they cut into the bag to get it. Why not just take the whole bag?" She raised an eyebrow at me. "It *was* on his shoulder like a purse."

"Guys, here's the problem. You think they're going to put

a laptop theft with nothing but fart jokes in it on the news?"
I said. "Do you know how much stuff probably gets stolen
here?"

Some dude chimed in, "A lot. I just stole this!" He held
up Thor's hammer.

I didn't want to tell him that it had been in my butt
cheeks.

"Let's track down that blood trail," I said.

As we walked down the hallway past the scene of the crime,
we stared at the floor, searching for any evidence we could
find. It was difficult navigating the traffic through the halls.
We were inspecting the floor inch by inch, following each
drop of dried blood to the next one. We came to an intersec-
tion of hallways, which amplified the difficulty level. First,
there were a lot more people. And second, it wasn't obvious
which direction they headed in. The trail of blood had been
to the right of the hall, sometimes straying a little toward the
center, but that path ended abruptly.

We searched for a few minutes. Then I found the trail
again. "I found something!" I yelled. Sophie, Ben, and
Sammie made their way over to me. I pointed to a tiny blood
stain. "Look. She must've cut across traffic," as a blue Orc
from Lord of the Rings stared me down while passing by.

Sammie scooted over a few feet and found another stain,
only a few feet from the wall on the left side of the hallway,
opposite from where the trail originally started.

Ben nodded to the garbage pail a few feet from us and
said, "I think you should check the garbage."

"Why me?" I asked.

"C.T. chose you to solve the case."

I shook my head. "He chose all of us." I took a deep breath. "Okay, I'll take a peek. No promises to touch anything."

A dude dressed as Batman walked up toward the garbage pail. He took off his mask, snorted one of the most disgusting sounds I've ever heard, as if summoning mucus from the depths of his soul, and hocked a loogie into the garbage.

"The real Bruce Wayne would never have done that," Sophie said.

"Right. I've suddenly changed my mind," I said. "What other options do we have?"

"Perhaps I could be of assistance?" a voice said, over my shoulder.

I turned around to find myself face to face with Superman, red boots and all. The hair curl could've been better and a clean shave wouldn't have hurt, but he looked the part of Superman, even if we all knew his muscles were foam.

"Did you happen to see a lady with a wig getting taken away by a security guard?" I asked.

"Yes, she came through here," Superman said. "What's the problem?"

Sophie asked, "Was she crazy?"

"Not really. Kind of quiet. I almost didn't notice them, but The Thing knocked her wig off, the clumsy rock, and spilled fruit punch or something on it."

"Did you get a look at her face?" I asked.

Superman frowned and asked, "No. Why are you tracking her?"

"We think she could've stolen something."

"All I can tell you is that some kid gave it back to her

while she was standing near here. I didn't really pay attention. I didn't know she was a criminal."

"Where's the kid?"

He shrugged.

I looked at the garbage pail and then back at Superman. "Can you use your X-Ray vision to look into the garbage can, so I don't have to search through it? It's kinda disgusting. Batman hocked a serious loogie in there."

Superman turned up his nose. "He's a disgusting creature. I don't know what the appeal is. But I'm sorry, guys. The X-Ray vision is not working today."

I scratched my head, thinking. "Hey, Superman, you ever think of getting a corporate soup sponsorship deal? Or maybe Super Glue? I'm more of a sandwich man myself, but to each his own," I said.

"How about Clark bars?" Ben added.

"Guys, this is really fun and all. But I'm thirty-eight years old. I live with my mother. My Lois Lane dumped me and I barely fit into these tights anymore."

"What does that have to do with anything?"

"I'm just cranky. I'm tired of the witty banter."

Sophie narrowed her eyes at him and said, "Your loss."

Superman tossed his cape off his shoulder and said, "Yeah, definitely. I'll regret it for the rest of my life."

"What a jerk," Sammie said. "You think you know someone..."

"Now what?" Ben asked.

"It's time to take this on for Team C.T." I stared at the garbage pail, willing myself to touch it. I leaned over the top and looked into it. And nearly vomited. I had no idea that superheroes or at least people pretending to be superheroes could be so disgusting. Batman's loogie was the least of my concerns. I'm not sure why there was a baby's diaper in there or why that baby seemed to have eaten too many tacos for breakfast, but it was there, nonetheless. I didn't know how to get past it.

"No," I said, shaking my head. "I love C.T. and all, but let's leave this to the professionals."

"Lose something, little fella?" a voice boomed from above me.

I looked up to see a heavily-muscled, shirtless dude, painted from head to toe in green, staring down at me.

"Yes, unfortunately, Hulk. My friend here lost her wig and somebody tossed it in there. Under the regurgitated cheese whiz."

The Hulk peered down at the garbage below. "That's the most infuriating thing I've ever seen. I'd just buy a new one."

"Yeah, it has sentimental value," I said, thinking on my feet.

"Hmmm," Hulk grunted. "Use these," he said, pulling off oversized green fists.

"Don't you need them?" Sophie asked.

I shot a look at her. I needed them, too.

The Hulk said, "They're kinda sweaty and I can't fix my hair with them. Gotta look good for the ladies, you know?"

I wondered why he would paint himself green if that was the case, but whatever. I had a plan to get the wig without getting loogie all over me.

"I look ridiculous," I said, holding the oversized fists up. "These are bigger than my head."

The Hulk chuckled and said, "It's going to look a lot worse when you start digging through the garbage with them."

I groaned, took a deep breath, and stared down into the garbage. I felt like I was playing a really strange game of Operation where, instead of hearing the buzzer go off if you made a mistake, you got taco tornado of a baby diaper all over you.

I held the diaper in one hand, softly holding it closed as best I could with my ridiculous hands, and grabbed the curly wig with my other. My concentration was approaching bomb-diffusion levels.

And then I was jolted back to Comic Con when C.T. yelled, "What's up, buddy?"

"Ahhh, farts!" I screamed, tossing the diaper across the hallway. I watched in slow motion as it rolled in mid-air, spraying contents in every direction on top of unsuspecting superheroes (or more like pooperheroes).

C.T. stood beside me, a sheepish look on his face.

"What now?" I asked.

C.T. yelled, "We run!"

CHAPTER 7

I tossed the Hulk hands up in the air and didn't look back. I heard a groan from behind me. I think I may have inadvertently punched someone in the face.

Sophie and Sammie took off running back to where we came from. We followed. There was no point figuring out what had happened to the diaper. There was no smoothing that over, no pun intended. Or wiping the slate clean, as they say. Pun intended.

Sophie and Sammie stopped near the scene of the original crime to let us all catch up. We were far enough away that it was likely no one had followed us. Most people probably didn't even know that they had poop splattered on them.

"Over here," C.T. whispered. He flashed a badge to a security guard standing outside an unmarked door. The guard opened the door and we all followed C.T. inside.

We were backstage in one of the panel discussion rooms. Half the lights were on and the room was empty.

I looked down at the wig to examine it. There was a little

piece of latex attached to the wig, right where the wearer's forehead would be. I thought about plucking it off, but had no interest in touching the thing without another oversized, green hand.

"What is that?" Ben asked. "Is it part of a mask?"

"Don't know. Looks like it," I said.

"It looks like latex from a Hollywood mask. Outside of the poop smell, I'd say it was very high quality stuff," C.T. said.

"Was the crazy lady even wearing a mask?" Sophie asked.

I shrugged. "I didn't think so at the time, but now I'm not sure."

C.T. said, "I didn't notice it, either."

"So, maybe this isn't even the suspect's mask," I said. "Somebody else could've thrown theirs out."

"But it's all we got, so we should explore it," Ben said.

"Half the people in this place are wearing latex something or other," C.T. said.

"So, first, was it hers?" I asked.

Sophie finished my thought. "And second, was it a disguise or a costume?"

"Why would it be in the garbage if she wasn't trying to fool us?" Ben asked.

I shrugged. "Didn't the sham of a Superman say The Thing knocked it off?"

"Yeah," Ben said, frowning.

C.T. said, "Hmm....Did anybody recognize the costume?"

We shook our heads.

"Is she in the pictures?" Ben asked Sophie.

"I thought we were never talking about them again?" I asked.

Sophie smirked. "I never agreed to that. Plus, they're crime scene photos now."

"Okay, so let's say she is the perpetrator, we don't know how she smuggled the laptop out of there. Her purse was smaller than C.T.'s."

"C.T.'s man bag," C.T. corrected.

I smiled and continued, "We don't know anything about what her motive is, if she even has one."

"And why was she taken away by security?" Ben asked.

"This is hard," C.T. whined.

"We've got nothing. Again," I said, dejected.

C.T. looked at his watch and said, "The panel is starting in thirty minutes. They're gonna start letting people in soon. This is a disaster. Thanks for the help, though." C.T. wiped his brow and said, "I've gotta get situated with Kyle and I need to talk to the moderator. I can't believe I agreed to do a panel with Jimmy O'Beans."

The crew reassembled at the panel discussion. Just Charles, Cheryl, and Luke didn't have any more luck than we did. Well, maybe a little. They didn't have to go fishing in a diaper-infested garbage pail for evidence of a possible suspect with no means of committing the crime or any known motive. We sat in the front row as fans settled into their seats.

C.T. stood up on the stage, off to the side, talking to Kyle. He was pacing around, agitated.

I listened as best I could to his conversation with Kyle. "To top it all off, Danielle couldn't get me on TV before Comic Con. We need the publicity."

"It's hard. I talked to her. There was nothing she could do. You don't have enough followers on Instagram. They just don't care about fart jokes."

"Well, they should. It's just that this is big. We worked so hard for this. I need it to work. We made a lot of promises.

How many journalists are coming to the press release later?"
C.T. asked.

Kyle looked down at his sneakers. "Four confirmed."

C.T.'s face dropped. "Four? Oh, man. This is terrible. Any
bloggers?"

"A couple."

"A couple?"

Kyle asked, "Why are you repeating everything?"

C.T. threw his hands up in the air. "Why am I repeating
everything?" he shrugged. "I actually have no idea."

My stomach swirled. I thought I might puke. My Sherlock Holmes-like brain was computing like mad. I leaned
over to Sophie and Ben and said, "I just had a terrible
thought."

"What?" Sophie asked.

I took a deep breath. I think Sophie might be right.

Ben's face registered confusion. "What do you mean?"

"I mean, what if it was all part of the plan? What if C.T. is
in on it?"

Ben said, "That's crazy."

Sophie said, "Maybe he needs money."

"Maybe he wants to hype the book sales," I added. "He
was just complaining to Kyle that they weren't getting
enough promotion. That they needed this launch to work."

We all looked up at C.T. again. I read his lips and heard
most of what he said. C.T. pointed to a banner behind the
empty chairs on the table. It had his face on it with a
thumbs up. "How much did that banner cost?"

"$300," Kyle said.

"300? Oh, sorry. I'm repeating again."

C.T. shrugged and started walking toward us.

"Oh, no," I whispered. "He's coming our way."

C.T. sat down on the edge of the stage right in front of us.

"Hey, guys. Something wrong?"

"No, just frustrated," I said.

C.T. looked over at Cheryl and Just Charles. "You find anything out, Ms. Van Snoogle-Something?"

"Not yet."

"Too bad. Have you met Kyle yet?" C.T. asked.

"Nope," I said.

C.T. waved Kyle over. Kyle walked over with a drink in his hand. He handed it to C.T. before sitting down next to him.

"Here's your tea," Kyle said.

"Thanks," C.T. said, before taking a sip.

"You drink tea?" I asked.

"Yeparoo."

"I love iced tea," Just Charles chimed in.

Sophie asked, "You don't drink coffee? I thought all adults did."

"Nope, not this one. Coffee comes from beans and beans make you fart. And not all regions I travel in have Barking Tree Frogs to blame for my farts."

"I knew it!" I yelled, jumping to my feet.

"Just kidding," C.T. said, while Kyle stifled a laugh. "It was totally Thor. I can't believe you guys don't believe me." C.T. looked at Kyle and said, "They're helping me with the investigation. Can you give them your card in case they need anything?"

"Sure. It's nice to meet you all," Kyle said, and then handed me a few business cards.

I passed them to the rest of the crew.

"There's the moderator," Kyle said, pointing behind us.

C.T. popped up. "Gotta go. I'll see you guys after the panel."

They walked away. As soon as they were out of ear shot, Sophie asked, "What if the assistant was involved in it?"

"Why would he be?" Ben asked. "C.T. seems like a good guy."

"Let's not get sentimental. He's a suspect," Sophie said.

CHAPTER 8

We all looked at each other. C.T. was a suspect.

"He is?" Ben asked, looking at me.

I shrugged. "It's possible. He has a potential motive in trying to drum up publicity for his new series. Plus, he had the opportunity. Don't you think it's weird that it took him so long to figure out his man bag was torn?"

Ben said, "I guess. There was a lot going on."

Sophie nodded and said firmly, "They're both suspects. We haven't ruled anyone out yet."

I wondered if she had watched too many police shows or something. She was taking this pretty seriously. I nodded to Ben. "It could've been you."

"Me?" he asked, defensively.

"Just kidding, dude," I said, smiling.

The panel was getting started. C.T. was seated in the middle of a three-person table. There was a twenty-something year-old man with a beard and glasses to his left and an empty seat to his right, which was seemingly meant for Jimmy O'Beans.

A woman with a blond ponytail, jeans, and a t-shirt

walked out to the podium that stood angled to face the panel. The crowd cheered as the panel was about to begin. The woman smiled and said, "Welcome to Comic Con! We are pleased to present our graphic novel panel, consisting of Marvel artist, Tommy Moore, author C.T. Walsh, and author Jimmy O'Beans, who does not appear to be here..." her voice trailed off.

"Where is he?" I asked. "Kind of a big deal to miss this, especially when you're not that good."

"You don't like his stuff?" Sophie whispered.

"He's okay. I liked him when I was younger."

The moderator looked off to the side of the stage while the crowd began to grumble. And then Jimmy made his entrance. On the side of the stage opposite the moderator, a man swung on a rope. It was Jimmy O'Beans! The crowd cheered, as Jimmy's cape flapped in the air. I wasn't sure if he was farting or if it was just his momentum.

Jimmy let go of the rope as he approached the center of the stage. His sneakers touched down with little turbulence and he slid to a stop. Most of the crowd stood and cheered. Jimmy bowed to the applause and then stood up.

"You're too kind! I don't deserve it. Oh, yes I do! I'm the Prince of Potty Humor!"

I looked over at C.T. He smirked and rolled his eyes. I was taken aback when half the crowd started farting. My crew and I turned around, trying to figure out what the heck was going on. Thankfully, a bunch of people in the crowd were making fart noises with their hands and armpits, and not actually farting. Had it been real, we all could've died. C.T. shook his head disapprovingly. I would've thought he would appreciate that kind of gesture. Maybe he was jealous.

C.T. leaned away from the microphone and looked off stage to Kyle and said, "Why don't I have a cape?"

"You never asked for one."

C.T. shook his head. "Can I please have a cape? I've always wanted one. Ever since I was a boy."

"Yes, sir."

"How fast can you get it here?"

Kyle shrugged. "There's a cape stand just around the corner, next to the animal hides and Viking helmets."

"Make sure it's cool, like with a velvet lining or something. It has to be dashing. It can't look like a kid's Halloween costume."

"Got it," Kyle said.

"Always second best," Jimmy said.

Jimmy walked over to the table, stared at C.T. and grabbed the mic in front of his own empty seat, as the crowd's cheers and faux farting faded. Without waiting for a question from the moderator, he introduced himself.

"Well, hello there! For those of you who don't know me- I have no idea why that would be- I am Jimmy O'Beans, the Prince of Potty Humor, author of The Colon Chronicles and Potty Pandemonium."

Everyone stared at Jimmy. C.T. looked up at Jimmy, unimpressed. "Would you care to sit down?" He didn't seem to like being upstaged.

Jimmy ignored C.T. and yelled into the microphone. "This is my outhouse!"

C.T. shook his head. "Dude, that's just weird."

"Stand up."

"What? Why? This is a panel discussion. What are you doing?"

"Stand up," Jimmy insisted.

C.T. rolled his eyes and stood up.

Jimmy smacked C.T. in the back of the head with the palm of his hand.

C.T. grabbed his head and said, "Oww! What's the deal, man?"

Jimmy made no apologies. He pandered to the crowd. "This rivalry has gone on for too long. It's time we end this here and now in front of the best fart fans in the world!"

"Fart fans, really?" C.T. asked, confused. But then C.T. leaned in. "Oh, do you want me to play along? We should totally have a fake rivalry like in WWE wrestling, to drum up ratings."

Jimmy face dropped, disappointed. "Fake? You don't hate me?"

"I totally hate you, dirt bag!" C.T. yelled to the crowd, and then pushed Jimmy on the shoulder. "Is that good?" he whispered. "This is awesome. You want to punch me in the face? The crowd'll love it. Be careful, though. I do throw a mean Camel Clutch."

Two police officers entered the back of the room and walked toward the stage. C.T. caught sight of them and said, "Dang it, man. Spoiled by the boys in blue again. Plus, I don't have my cape. Rain check, bro. You understand, right?"

Jimmy O'Beans shrugged.

"We're gonna do this," C.T. assured Jimmy. "And you're gonna get crushed. Care to sit down and discuss the world of fart jokes like civilized men until then?"

"I guess," Jimmy slipped into his seat, disappointed.

"I'm gonna kick his butt later!" C.T. yelled to the crowd.

Tommy looked at the moderator, confused.

She just shrugged.

For a fart jokes panel, it was less than explosive. Well, at least after the modest kerfuffle between C.T. and Jimmy.

After the panel was over, we all stood up and cheered. My Spidey Senses tingled when I saw two more police officers hanging out by the side of the stage. The original two that had entered were walking up the stairs to the stage. I wasn't sure who they were interested in talking to. I assumed it was to give C.T. an update.

I heard Sergeant Villone say to C.T., "You're coming with us. We have some questions."

"Okay," C.T. said, shrugging nonchalantly.

"You don't understand. We're taking you in."

"I'm with you," C.T. said, seemingly not understanding what the cops were insinuating.

I looked over to my crew. "Guys, we have a huge problem."

"What's that?" Just Charles said.

"We think C.T. is the thief."

Just Charles nearly fell over. "Why did you have to go and ruin Comic Con?"

"What are you talking about?" Luke asked, confused.

I looked back up at C.T. He was still talking to the officers. Kyle had joined the conversation. The rest of the stage had cleared out, except Jimmy, who watched from the side of the stage.

"Wait, am I being detained?" C.T. asked, surprised.

"No," the officer said evenly. "Unless you're not gonna come quietly." The officer cracked his neck and then his knuckles.

C.T gulped. "You think I did this? What is going on here? My laptop was stolen. Why would I do it myself?"

"Let's go."

C.T.'s face registered shock. It was ghost white. He turned to Kyle. "Call my lawyer." And then to us. "Guys, I need your help. I didn't do this. You gotta believe me."

CHAPTER 9

As C.T. was being escorted off the stage by Officer Yasmanian, I called up to Sergeant Villone. "Sir, what's going on?"

Sergeant Villone huffed and then walked over to me. He

smirked and said, "It looks like the author set the whole thing up for publicity. Did you see how he tried to create that rivalry?"

C.T. was escorted off the stage and out the back of the auditorium, four officers guarding him.

I hadn't been that disappointed in a long time. I couldn't believe it. I mean, it made sense, but still, it didn't register.

My crew crowded around me, as C.T. disappeared.

Just Charles said, "This doesn't make any sense. What was he talking about?"

"I heard C.T. complaining about the lack of publicity for his appearance today. And it took so long for him to figure out his laptop was missing. I'm not sure he ever had it. Maybe his bag was cut the whole time and he just threw the box cutter on the floor. I don't know," I said, shaking my head.

We moped around Comic Con for about thirty minutes, just looking at movie props, costumes, and other cool merch that was not in my middle school student budget. I thought about calling my dad and having him pick us up, but I knew he was busy at his meeting.

Sophie grabbed my hand and pulled me aside. "Are you okay?" she asked, her eyes filled with concern.

"Not really. How could he do this? I mean, I guess I could see how there could be some motivation for him to do it, but he's already popular. He sells a lot of books. He's on a panel at Comic Con. Does it really make sense for him to risk that just to sell a few more books?"

She shrugged. "I don't know. Greed is a funny thing. I'm not really sure what that means, but my grandmother used to say it after stealing my dessert."

I threw my bag down on the floor. The rest of the crew walked over with concern on their faces.

"This doesn't sit right with me," I said. "We didn't come here to pretend to be detectives. We came here to have fun at Comic Con."

"Yeah, but he said he didn't do it. He asked for our help," Ben said.

"A lot of criminals say they didn't do it," Sammie said.

"Yeah, but I believe him," Cheryl said.

"Me, too," Luke added.

"I'm not willing to give up just yet," Ben said.

Ben looked at me. "You're giving up on him?"

"No," I said, annoyed.

"Okay, what about the rest of you?" Ben asked, excitedly.

Sophie said, "I'm in, but in for what? The professionals say he's guilty."

"Well, let's make sure," Ben said.

"How are we gonna do that?" I asked.

Cheryl took a deep breath. "What info could they possibly have found to arrest him? They didn't say they had the laptop. They didn't say there was anyone else involved."

"So what? We're gonna bust him out?" Sophie asked.

"A prison break sounds awesome, but I have to meet Wonder Woman for lunch," Luke said, sheepishly.

"I think we have to prove him right," I said.

Sammie threw her hands up. "But how? What can we figure out what the cops haven't?"

"Not sure," I held the errrr, as I thought and then it popped into my head, "Sherlock. We're goin' full on detective, Dr. Watson," I said to Sophie.

"Why am I the sidekick?" Sophie asked. "You don't know anything about my detective skills to demote me to sidekick. I think I should be Sherlock Holmes."

"I'm terribly sorry about my faux pas," I said, softly.

"Let's just work together...And by the way, my mistake was something Sherlock would totally do."

Sophie just shook her head.

"What about the lady in the wheel chair?" I asked.

"She has a name," Sophie said, annoyed. "It's Sara Finkle. You're a real attention-to-detail kinda guy, Sherlock," she said, with a smirk.

"That's hurtful," I said, feigning sadness.

"Could she have slid the laptop underneath her chair and wheeled it out of there?" Ben asked.

"I guess it's possible. But she was the last one off the floor. Her chair was upside down," I said.

"I don't see how anybody could've hidden anything in there," Just Charles said. "I was right on top of her. I think she gave me a purple nurple when we were on the floor."

"How can we find Ms. Finkle?" Cheryl asked.

"Why don't we just page her to the security desk?" Just Charles asked.

I shrugged. "I guess it's worth a shot. I think there's one near the scene of the diaper disaster."

"We're going back there?" Ben asked. "They might have our pictures on the wall."

"They have enough to worry about," I said. "We'll be fine."

"We shouldn't all interrogate her. It'll be seven against one. She'll clam up," Sophie said.

I nodded. "Anybody want to interrogate her?"

"Not me," Ben said. "She packs a pretty serious punch."

"Yeah. I'm out, too. Cheryl should. She's an investigative reporter," Just Charles said.

Cheryl stared him down.

Just Charles changed his mind. "I'd love to participate. A few steps behind everyone else."

Sophie looked at me. "You should do it, too. C.T. asked you to help."

"He asked all of us to help," I said, defensively.

Sophie didn't respond. She used silence as a weapon.

I caved. "Okay. I'll do it."

CHAPTER 10

Ms. Finkle rolled up to the security booth. The officer in charge nodded in our direction. She spun around in her chair and rolled her eyes. Then she rolled the rest of herself toward us.

"What do you want?" she asked, annoyed.

I decided to use the interrogation techniques of one Principal Buthaire, also known as Prince Butt Hair or simply, Butt Hair. He would always hold the r when saying my name, like Misterrrrrrr Davenport. I felt it was appropriate to use in this context. "Misssssss Finkle, we've been tasked with solving the laptop theft of one C.T. Walsh, aka the Shakespeare of Fart Jokes."

Cheryl shook her head and cut in, "Did you see anything suspicious before or after the people pileup with C.T.?"

"No."

"Did you do anything suspicious?" I asked.

"Not that I'm aware of."

I leaned down and peered under her wheel chair. "Does your wheelchair have any secret compartments, Misssssss Finkle?"

"Well, if I tell you, they wouldn't be secret now, would they?"

"Touché. Misssss Finkle, Do you have a fake leg that could perhaps fit a lap top?"

"Why do you keep saying my name like that?"

I scoffed. "It's how you say people's names when you're suspicious of them. Everybody knows that."

"Nobody knows that," she said, frowning.

"That's what people who don't know say."

"Are we finished? This is ridiculous. I have a date with Wolverine."

"No, we have a few more questions," Cheryl said.

"Okay, I'll humor you. You think I stole the laptop? Where would I put it?"

"Your secret compartment," I said.

"I don't have one."

"Do you have an invisibility cloak?" I asked.

"I'm not Harry Potter. Guys, I know you're trying to help, but I didn't take anything. How could I have done this?"

"You're right," I said. "Sorry to bother you. If you see anything suspicious, please let us know."

She wheeled herself back away from us. And then I saw something. And it was suspicious. The bottom of her shoes were worn down. The rubber on the bottom was so thin, I thought I might be able to poke through it with a pencil. Grimmwolf the Gopher, our fearless and often overly-aggressive mascot at Cherry Avenue Middle School, probably could've chewed through it in a second. True, he might be able to chew through metal, but still, they were thin.

"Thank you for your time, Missssss Finkle." I said, turning away from her and then back toward her, quickly. "Oh, there is just one last thing. If you're in a wheelchair because you can't walk, why are the bottom of your shoes worn to the soles? Confess that you stole the laptop and we'll let you off easy!"

Miss Finkle shook her head and said, "They're hand-me-downs."

"Hand-me-whats? Hand-me-downs?" I asked.

"I don't like to pay for shoes, being that I don't really use them, so I get them from friends. After they use them."

"Oh. I feel sheepish."

"Nice job, Sherlock," Sophie said from behind me.

I shot her a look and then turned back to Miss Finkle. I smiled and waved. "Have a great day! Enjoy the show!"

"If you were adults, I'd drop every last one of you like a toilet seat," she said, peeling out.

"I want to be Sherlock now," Luke said.

"What would you do?" Sophie asked, doubtfully.

Luke paced, thinking. "Well, that Kyle guy seems nefarious."

"Yeah, he's totally guilty," Sammy said. "He's the jealous assistant."

Ben added. "He wants C.T.'s success for his own."

"Really?" I asked.

Luke shrugged. "I don't know, but we should check him out."

"Let's call him," I said, taking out my phone and Kyle's business card.

"Maybe we shouldn't take such a hard approach next time," Cheryl said. "People don't like to be accused of crimes."

"Yeah, I totally understand that," I said, remembering how many times I had found my innocent self in Principal Butt Hair's office.

I dialed the phone. "Hello, Kyle? It's Austin. C.T. introduced us at the panel discussion...We're okay...Can you meet up at the food court? Okay, we'll see you there in ten minutes. Make sure you're not followed."

"Aren't you being a little dramatic?" Sammie asked.

I hung up the phone. "You guys are no fun. How often do we get to work a mystery for our favorite author?"

We navigated the crowds and wacky costumes and made it to the food court in less than ten minutes. Kyle was waiting for us near the condiment table.

As we approached Kyle, Luke looked around and asked, "Do I have to pay for something if I just want to eat the pickles?"

"Have at it, bro," I said.

"Sweet! This is awesome!" Luke yelled. He was a real asset to the detective team.

I whispered to Ben, "Look at him, looking around so suspiciously."

"You told him to make sure he wasn't followed."

"True, but still."

I waved to Kyle as we walked toward him. He nodded to an empty table and headed toward it. We sat down at the long table and settled in. We were gonna play it cool.

"Any updates on C.T.?" I asked.

Kyle shook his head. "No. His lawyer is on the way. I haven't had any contact with him. Did you guys find anything?"

Cheryl said, "We interrogated that Sara Finkle lady."

Kyle's eyes widened. "That's brave of you. I heard about how she wielded Thor's hammer."

"We don't think she did it," Sophie said. "She didn't have a way to get the laptop out of there, plus she stuck around to wait for security and the cops. There was no place to hide it."

"That's all we got," I said. "So, C.T. is probably going to federal prison for the next thirty years."

"Don't beat yourself up, guys. We'll figure it out. He's not going away for thirty years. Twenty, maybe."

My eyes bulged.

"Just kidding," Kyle said, laughing.

I exhaled, relieved.

Sophie asked, "How did you get involved with C.T.?"

"It was simple enough," Kyle said. "He put out an ad for an author assistant. I had worked for a few authors before. We clicked. I've been working for him for a few years now."

"Did you ever want to write?" Cheryl asked.

"Not really. It's not my skill set."

"It must be fun working for a successful author," Ben said.

"Yeah, it's been great," Kyle said. "No complaints. Well, except for the fact that my boss is under arrest."

"Who do you think stole the laptop?" I asked.

"I don't have a clue. I wasn't there. I only know what you and C.T. think."

"We don't have a suspect."

"And I know it's not C.T.," Kyle said, firmly.

"Are you sure?" Sophie asked.

"Yes."

"He didn't do it for the publicity?" Just Charles asked.

"He wouldn't do that. He'd rather sell zero books than cheat or break the law."

"So, we have a big old fart burger with beans on top," I said.

"What the heck does that mean?" Sophie asked.

"It means we got nothing," Kyle said.

"You speak fart burger?" Ben asked.

"I work for the Shakespeare of Fart Jokes. Fluency in fart burger is required."

Sophie shook her head and took out her phone.

"Who are you calling?" I asked.

"I'm not."

"Texting?"

"I want to look at the pictures of your nose hair again," she said, straight-faced.

"Had I known how often you were going to check out my nose hair, I would've styled it with some gel. Or a wet, little boogie," I said.

"That's gross," Sophie said, scrolling through her pictures. "Yeah, I really love this pic. I'm gonna frame it and put it next to your Batman underwear pic from Santukkah!"

Kyle looked confused.

"Be careful, people might think you're a little crazy with your Austin shrine."

Kyle looked at us and said, "You guys are weird. It's no wonder you hit it off with C.T."

"You think we hit it off with C.T.?" Ben asked, excitedly.

"Oh, definitely. He didn't ask anyone else to help him." Kyle paused for a moment and then continued, "He does blame his farts on pretty much anybody he can, so don't read too much into that, though."

I slapped the table. "This stinks. Not the fart stuff. The rest of this whole thing."

Sophie was still looking at all the pictures.

"Guys, isn't it weird that with all that happened, the security guard didn't wait for any backup and just took the crazy lady away?" I asked.

Cheryl agreed, "Yeah, why her?"

"The other guy was just as crazy, yelling at C.T.," Ben said. "Even C.T. said he thought it was weird."

Sophie looked closer at her phone and then zoomed in and up on one of the pictures. "Wait. One. Second."

"What is it?" Sammie asked.

"Look at this," Sophie said, holding the phone in the center of the table for us all to see. We all leaned in.

"See the security guard here? That's who took the crazy lady away."

"Yeah, so?" Luke said.

"She's not wearing the same hat as the other security guards." Sophie smiled at me. "Sophie Holmes, at your service."

"Nice work, Ms. Holmes," I said.

Sophie continued, "I don't remember exactly what the second crew of security guards was wearing, but it was different."

"You're right," I agreed. "And remember, they didn't

know that there was a crazy lady. They all had radios attached to their shoulders."

Sophie moved the picture to focus on the security guard's shoulder. "This one didn't."

"This is huge," Ben said.

Cheryl pointed across the food court. "Look at those two over there eating lunch and look at the uniform in the picture."

"Oh, wow," Kyle said. "Different shoulder patches, different hats, no walkie-talkie."

"So, what does this mean?" Sammie asked.

"I think it means that the crazy wig lady and the security guard were in on the heist together. The woman jumped on C.T., stole his laptop, and the security guard helped her get the laptop and herself out of there. Am I missing anything?"

"Don't think so," Sophie said.

"It's a great plan," Ben said. "Start a commotion, steal the bag, and then have a getaway planned. Nobody would stop the security guard from taking her away."

"Remember C.T. asked why he was taking the woman away? He told him nobody was to blame, but the guard removed her anyway," I said.

"You guys are good," Kyle said.

"So, now what? How do we find out who they are?" Cheryl asked.

"What would the police do?" Just Charles said.

"Run her face through a database or something and see if they had a match on her," I said. My dad watched a lot of police shows.

Ben shook his head. "We don't have those resources."

"What if there's an app for it," Sammie asked.

"You think?" Cheryl asked.

"There's an app for everything," I said. "There's an app

that you can fake shave your face with. I think Derek uses it to pretend he has a mustache."

"I had an app where you could milk a cow," Kyle said. "It was fun."

"Dude, that's weird," Luke said.

Just Charles took out his phone. He was our tech genius. I was pretty good, but he was better. He said, "Let's see what we have." He scrolled through his phone. "Here's a social media facial recognition app. We can crop that picture and enter it on the app. If there's a match, it will show us her social media profiles."

"Let's do it," I said.

Sophie air dropped the picture to Just Charles, while he downloaded the app.

"My dad is gonna kill me if I go over on data," Just Charles said. His phone dinged. He saved the pic to his photo folder and opened the app. "Let's see what we get." He uploaded the photo to the app and hit search with his fingers crossed.

"Let me have a copy of that picture," Kyle said. "I'll circulate it around and give it to the cops. We'll see if we can't get to the bottom of this."

"So now what? C.T. is locked up, but innocent. How do we get him out?" I asked.

"We wait," Just Charles said. "It's still searching."

Kyle said, "Got it. I'll take this to them now." He stood up and said, "Good work. Keep me in the loop if you find anything out."

"I don't want to wait," I said.

"What can we do?" Sophie asked.

"Well, we broke out of prison once," I said, referring to the escape room prison we broke out of at a Renaissance

Fair. "It's gotta be easier to break someone out than to break out when you're already in."

"I'm confused," Sophie said, frowning.

"Me, too," I said.

"And that was a fake prison," Just Charles said.

"True, but with some military-grade explosives it should be a piece of cake," Luke said.

"Yeah, I've got some in my backpack," I said, picking my backpack up from the floor. I stood up and said, "Let's do this!"

CHAPTER 11

I would not be doing this. Whatever *this* was. Sophie and Sammie shrieked, as two blurs surged at me.

The blurs collided with me like two Mack trucks. Bones crunched. Bruises were brewing. And pain. There was a lot of pain. I found myself in another heap of people. It was a problem at Comic Con that I was unaware of prior to attending.

"Get off him!" Sophie yelled, smacking a security guard on the shoulder.

"Back up!" Benson, the over zealous security guard, yelled.

"Secure the bag!" the other guard, Fischer, yelled.

My ribs were massaged with the guards' fists a few times before I parted with my bag. Fischer clutched it with both hands.

"What's...going...on?" I said through gasps.

The guards ignored him. "Implement bomb protocol."

"What?" I yelled, struggling to my feet. I felt like Flat Stanley, the book character that got squashed by his cork board. This was surely worse. "It was a joke," I said. "Open the bag and see. It's all snacks!"

"Do not open that bag! We're gonna have to evacuate and call the bomb squad," Fischer said.

"No!" I yelled.

"And you're coming with us," Benson said, grabbing my

arms and spinning me around. "You got cuffs?" he asked his partner.

"No. Why don't they trust us with cuffs? Here we are saving the world, but no, we're not responsible enough to carry a pair of handcuffs," Fischer said.

Sophie saw an opening as the guards complained. Fischer held the bag in one hand, the backpack dangling next to his knee. She rushed him and snatched the backpack out of his hand. She got some distance from them and pulled the zipper, but it was stuck.

Fischer rushed Sophie, his eyes filled with fire. She faked left and then cut right, Fischer falling for it. He crashed into an empty chair and toppled over it.

Benson seemingly didn't know what to do. He had me subdued and was probably reluctant to let me go, but also wanted to get his hand on the sugar/bomb in my backpack.

Sammie helped Sophie get the backpack open. The zipper flew open. Together, they turned the backpack over and emptied its contents onto the floor. Snack after snack fell out of the backpack, piling up on the floor in a fabulous display of sugar-filled treats. Had C.T. not been incarcerated, he probably would've tried to steal a few before they hit the ground.

"See! No bomb. Just sugar!" Sophie yelled.

Benson looked down at the pile of pleasure and shook his head. "We're gonna get in trouble...again."

Fischer wobbled to his feet, rubbing his head. "I think my vision's blurry, Chet."

"No, your vision is fine. That's just a lot of snacks. Unfortunately, none of them look like they can take down the convention center."

I thought his priorities might've been a little out of whack. It was most likely a good thing nobody was trying to bomb the place, but I wasn't about to say anything. I still wasn't sure if I was going to be arrested or not.

Benson forced a smile. "No harm. No foul. Sorry about the confusion, kids. You go on your way. We'll go on our way. Nobody writes any negative reports about anyone and we'll all be just fine."

Just Charles said, "That sounds fair."

Sophie handed me my backpack.

"Man, my zipper is broken. I hate that."

"Would you rather have been arrested for having a bomb?" Fischer asked.

"No. Thanks for that perspective," I said.

"No problem. We're here to serve."

"Yeah, serve my ribs some cracks," I said, rubbing my side. "As a penalty, you're gonna have to tell us where the police are holding C.T. Walsh."

Fischer shrugged. "Deal. There's a big room that they have. I think it's room D. Around the corner, down at the end," he said, pointing past the food court.

"Great. Thanks."

"Just a word of advice, kid. Don't joke about having explosives in your bag."

"That's some of the best advice I've ever gotten. Thank you."

"Have fun, guys," Benson said.

"We're going to break C.T. out of prison," Luke said.

Fischer dove for Luke like a football linebacker trying to sack the quarterback. He connected with Luke's shoulder. They both went down like a ton of bricks.

"It was a joke!" Luke yelled.

Fischer got up and dusted himself off. Benson helped Luke to his feet.

Benson smiled sheepishly. "Ha, what a funny misunderstanding. Just head right that way," he said, pointing, and then whispered to Fischer, "Dude, you're already on probation. You gotta stop tackling everyone."

CHAPTER 12

We arrived at Room D. There was an officer sitting at a table just inside the door. He was filling out paperwork as Sophie and I walked in. Officer Chulo looked up at me and frowned.

"Here to bail someone out?" he asked, gruffly.

"Kind of," I said. "I need to speak to Sergeant Villone about the C.T. Walsh case he's working on."

"Is that so?" Officer Chulo asked.

"Very so," Sophie said. "We've..." she looked at me and smirked before continuing, "cracked the case."

"Oh, I'm sure he can't wait to discuss it with you," Officer Chulo said, sarcastically.

I looked around the room. There were lines of people, mostly men in costumes, sitting on chairs, handcuffed to a long bar running in front of them.

After a moment, Sergeant Villone met us at the front table and looked at us curiously.

"Can I help you, kids? Officer Chulo said that you cracked the case I cracked two hours ago?"

"You're wrong," I said, simply.

"Oh, really?" Sergeant Villone said with a chuckle. He took his glasses off and wiped them clean. "How so?"

Sophie asked, "Have you checked the security tapes?"

"Not yet," he said. "Don't need to, though."

"Nice work," Sophie said, sarcastically. "There was a fake security guard." She reached for her phone and swiped it open. She held her phone out for the sergeant to see the picture.

"C.T. tried to get him to stop. Said the lady didn't do anything wrong, but they left anyway. We think the woman took the laptop, gave it to the security guard, and he helped her escape," I said, crossing my arms.

"Oops," Sergeant Villone said.

"What do you mean, 'oops'?" I asked.

"That changes things. Please give that picture to Officer Chulo here and I'll be right back."

Sophie did as she was told. After a few minutes, Sergeant Villone returned with C.T. He was uncuffed and looked like nothing had happened.

"You're free to go," Sergeant Villone said.

C.T. smirked at him and said sarcastically, "Thanks for the hospitality. Don't think you're getting a good review on Yelp from me."

"Oh, please don't go lower than three stars," Sergeant Villone pleaded.

"You should think of that before you just start arresting innocent people," C.T. said, angrily. "Two stars!" He held up three fingers.

"That's three," Officer Chulo said.

C.T. frowned and fixed his fingers. "Two stars!" He looked at Sophie and me and said, "Let's get out of here before we get arrested for poor math skills."

"That's not even a crime," Officer Chulo said. "At least I don't think it is." He scratched his head, thinking.

We walked out to smiles from the rest of the crew and Kyle, who had apparently shown up while we were freeing C.T.

"What happened?" Kyle asked.

"These guys freed me and we have a lead on the thief," C.T. said, engulfing us all in a giant hug.

When we broke from the hug, I had to ask, "Why are you gonna give them two stars on Yelp? Seems too high."

"The decor was decent. The chairs were kinda comfy." C.T. ran his fingers through his hair and took a deep breath. "The good news is that I made some new friends in there. The bad news is that I'm not sure any of them are gonna be out for another few years." He looked at me and my crew. "Thanks, guys. I knew I could count on you."

I tried to hide my guilt, but I don't think I did a very good job.

C.T. looked at me and asked, "What's wrong, Austin?"

"Well, to be honest, there was a time we thought you were the ringleader. But then we realized the security guard was a fake and you didn't know anything about it. I'm sorry," I said, hanging my head.

"I can understand how you might think I was doing it for my own gain. I could create a whole bunch of drama around the missing laptop and then miraculously get it back with big fanfare and then I could release the books. It was never at risk of piracy or being released to the public for free." C.T. paused for a moment and then continued, annoyed, "Man, we should've totally done that." He looked at us and said, "But I promise you I didn't do it. Do you think I would ruin this fabulous man bag just to sell a few more books?" He patted the bag on his shoulder. "Do you know how many books I'd have to sell just to afford a new one of these?"

"Fifty?" Sophie asked.

"Yeah, that's not that many," C.T. said, sheepishly.

Cheryl said, "You're not makin' a great case here."

Sophie asked, "You're still using it? Your purse?"

"This man bag? Yeah, well, I don't keep backups around. I only do that with underwear."

"You have backup underwear?" Ben asked.

"Sometimes. You never know, kids. You. Never. Know."

"Okay, that's just weird," I said, but then I remembered that I had worn a diaper to Sophie's house in sixth grade, so I wasn't exactly the most unweird guy.

C.T. sighed. "But maybe I should get a new one, because stuff keeps falling out. I lost my backup underwear a minute ago. Did you see a pair of boxers with pink polka dots?"

"Well, I'm sorry again," I said.

"No sweat, guys. Most Tuesdays, I think Kyle's a criminal and you don't see me beating myself up, do ya?"

"I guess not," I said. "I'm still not happy you tried to blame your farts on me," I said, trying to hold in a smile, and perhaps a tiny fart.

C.T. scoffed. "I would never do that to you. Thor? Maybe. Jimmy O'Beans? Definitely."

"We all would," Cheryl said. "That guy's an idiot."

C.T. looked at Kyle and asked, "You staying out of trouble?"

"It's not Tuesday, so I'm okay. It's good to have you back, sir."

I asked C.T., "Who do you think did it?"

"That lady was pretty crazy, but her lady bag was smaller than my man bag."

"Nobody uses the term lady bag," Sophie said.

"Well, they should."

"Did you see her butt?" I asked.

"Is that a trick question? I'm married, dude."

"Yeah, why are you asking about her butt?" Sophie asked, annoyed.

"Thor's hammer."

"Her butt looked like Thor's hammer?" C.T. asked. "I wish I'd seen that."

Sophie ignored him. "You think she smuggled a laptop with her butt?"

"It's a long shot, I admit... What about Thor?" I asked.

"Why would the Thunder God need a laptop?" Luke asked.

"I don't know," I said. "What's the economic cycle looking like in Asgard? Are they in a recession? And Thor's beard could've hidden the laptop. He had half a burrito spread out in that thing."

"What do you think, C.T.?" Cheryl asked.

"I write fart jokes for a living, guys. I'm not that smart."

"Don't beat yourself up. You write great fart jokes. You're fart smart," I said.

"Fart smart. I like the sound of that," C.T. said, smiling.

Ben said, "I can burp the alphabet. Do you want to hear?"

"I can do that, too! We can do it together," C.T. said, and then started.

After C.T. and Ben finished burping the alphabet, C.T. said, "This has been a great day."

Kyle asked, "Even with the laptop getting stolen?"

C.T.'s smile disappeared. "Oh yeah. No, but if I pretend that didn't happen, it's pretty good. I did kinda get arrested, too, which was a lowlight, if I'm being honest. I made a few new friends in there, though. I'm pretty certain they were all guilty of something, but still, I might keep in touch. That dude, Blister, was a really sweet guy."

"Why did they call him Blister?" Sammie asked, disgusted.

"You don't want to know," C.T. said.

Sophie asked C.T. "Any ideas on who would do this to you?"

"I've got nothing," he answered, shaking his head.

"Any death threats?" I asked.

"No. None."

"That's unfortunate," I said.

"Well, I guess it depends on how you look at it," C.T. said.

"Any enemies you can think of at all?" Cheryl asked.

C.T. said, "Guys, I'm a really likable guy. I just don't have any enemies."

"Personally, I think Randy did it," I said.

Just Charles said, "He's not even here!"

"Oh, right. Principal Butt Hair?" I countered.

"Nope."

"Your principal's name is Butt Hair? That's spectacular!" C.T. said, excitedly.

"Well, it's not his given name. We gave it to him."

"And we named our other principal, Armpit Hair," Luke added.

"You are the coolest kids I've ever met. Who's Randy?"

"The least coolest kid I've ever met," I said, disgustedly.

"He's an idiot," Ben added.

"Sounds like Jimmy O'Beans."

"What's that guy's deal?" Sophie asked.

"He's kinda harmless," C.T. shrugged. "Just a little full of himself."

"I really think he wants to punch you in the face," Kyle said.

"Well, that would be more than harmless. Why would he want to do that?" I asked.

C.T. waved it off. "He's a bit of drama king, but he's not a bad guy. We're competitors, but I don't think he is involved. Ugh. This is frustrating. What would Sherlock do?"

"We have that movie meeting," Kyle said to C.T.

"Yeah, and we're running out of time to get my laptop back. I think I have an idea," C.T. said. He looked at Kyle. "Like better than the fart-suppressing underwear idea."

"We almost did a science fair project on that!" Ben yelled.

"Maybe we should put our heads together on that one," C.T. said.

Kyle interrupted, "Umm, the laptop?"

"Oh, right. My idea. Totally forgot it." He thought for a minute, then continued, "So, anyway. We have the crazy lady and the security guard. Do we think the angry fan or the grumpy dude are involved?"

"That lady in the wheelchair had some anger issues, too," I said, "but we questioned her and came up empty."

C.T. shook his head. "Poor Thor. The guy got his clock cleaned. Nobody wants their signature weapon used against them." He turned to Kyle. "I totally need a signature weapon."

"Your signature weapon is the fart joke," Kyle answered.

"It is! You're the best sidekick around, Kyle! You're getting a bonus...high five! Sorry, until we get the laptop back, no cash bonuses."

We all cringed. We were not big on high fives. Thankfully, they kept the high five to themselves.

C.T. looked at his watch. "Okay, really have to go. I have a meeting with some movie execs."

"Really? That's super cool," Sammie said.

"Yep. I'm pitching them my screenplay, Fartopia."

We all looked at him like he was crazy.

C.T. continued, "It's gonna be the first movie that offers smells- we're gonna call it Fart-D."

"For Fart Dimension?" Sophie asked, disgustedly.

"That's awesome," Ben said.

"Aren't all the smells gonna be all farts, though?" I asked.

"Mostly, yeah," C.T. said, nodding.

"And people are gonna pay to smell farts?" Just Charles asked.

C.T. shrugged. "Maybe? It's a work in progress, but now I'm not as enthused as I was before." He looked at Kyle. "I think this is gonna stink, no pun intended." C.T. pointed to a man dressed as Batman. "What if I pitch them a series called Fartman? There could be a Fartmobile. He could stun enemies with a sonic fart gun."

"I'd definitely see that," Luke said.

"If we get it made, you guys are all executive producers on the project!" C.T. yelled. "Let's do this, Kyle!"

C.T. took off running down the hallway, enthusiastically.

Kyle rolled his eyes. "C.T.! This way!"

C.T. turned around and ran back the other way, past us, his enthusiasm still intact. "We're still doin' this!"

"That dude is weird," Just Charles said.

As we watched C.T. run by, Sophie asked, "Do you think Jimmy O'Beans could be involved? He's the only person who doesn't seem to like C.T."

Ben said, "He wasn't even there. I get that he doesn't seem to like C.T., but shouldn't we be sticking to the people who were there?"

"You make a good point," Sophie said. "C.T. is so likable."

"What's the motivation?" Cheryl asked. "Why take a high profile person and steal his stuff? I can't imagine the perp thought C.T. was a random person."

"If he was targeted, how did they know what was in his bag?" Ben asked.

"They could've seen him packing it up somewhere else," I said. And then Just Charles' pocket dinged. "What was that?" I asked.

"Let's see." Just Charles took out his phone and said, "We've got a notification on the facial recognition app."

"This could be our big break!" Sophie yelled.

CHAPTER 13

We all clustered around Just Charles.

"Grumpy Dude has a real name," Just Charles said, excitedly.

"Awww, man. I kinda liked Grumpy Dude," I said. "But solving the case is good, too."

"His name is Phil Grimes. Sounds like a grumpy dude."

"Was he even involved with the crazy lady and the security guard?" Cheryl asked.

"Who knows? I didn't see them talking at all," I said. "Anything on the security guard?"

Just Charles scrolled through the app. "No, looks like it's still searching. It wasn't a great picture of her."

"How do we find Phil Grimes, the Grumpy Dude?" I asked.

"We can start by asking around," Sophie said.

Just Charles turned around to see two dudes, dressed as Batman and Ironman. "Let's start with these two." He walked over to them as they spoke animatedly. Just Charles held his phone up to Batman's face. "Have you seen this man? He's evil."

I added, "He's my Joker." I thought Batman might have some empathy for us. It turned out no.

Batman grunted, "Not now kid. I'm in the middle of a conversation here."

"Not much of a conversation," Ironman said. "I've got so many more billions than you, there's nothing to debate."

Batman shook his head, too angry to respond.

"Guys, neither of you is a real billionaire. Can you please help us?" I pleaded.

Iron Man looked down at me, and pointed his palm repulsers at me, seemingly ready to blast me to smithereens.

"Yeah, well, I'll let you guys figure it out. We've got some place to be. Anywhere but here," I said, walking backward, slowly.

"What about security? We can page him," Sammie said.

"Worked before," Ben said.

I stood in front of the security desk. A young woman sat behind the desk, reading a magazine.

"Excuse me, ma'am?" I said.

She looked up at me, unenthused.

"I was hoping you can page my father. We got separated. His name is Grump, er Phil Grimes. He's going to be even grumpier when he sees me. Please don't tell him I'm here, though. He'll want to teach me a lesson."

She looked at me weirdly. Or perhaps, it was that she just thought I was weird. "Step aside and I'll take care of it. And don't ever call me ma'am again."

"No problem. Thanks."

I walked back to my crew and waited.

A few minutes later, Phil Grimes arrived, looking more confused than grumpy. It was definitely a better look. His shoulders slumped when he saw us.

"What do you want? How do you even know my name?"

"It's written on your cape. I read it when I was choking on it in the pile up."

"No, it's not."

"We're just doing some routine police work, trying to find a stolen laptop. We need to ask you a few questions," I said, firmly.

"This is ridiculous. If I stole the laptop, why would I still be here? I would be in Mexico or something. Or at least at my hotel."

It was a good point.

Sophie said, "Maybe because you don't want to seem suspicious by leaving."

I asked, "How did you know it was a laptop?"

"You said you were looking into the stolen laptop," he said, annoyed. "I'm outta here. I don't have time for this."

I really didn't know what to say. There was no evidence he was even involved. And he wasn't cooperating. "We're also still looking into your cutting of the line and bullying children, so don't leave the country."

"I'll be sure to not listen to anything you have to say."

"That's why they call him Grumpy Grimes," I said to my crew.

Grumpy Grimes turned around and stared us down. "Hey, how did you even know who I was?"

"It's our job to know." I stole the line from Max Mulvihill, my bathroom attendant and friend back at middle school.

Grumpy Grimes said, "I don't even want to know. Don't ever page me again." He turned and walked away, his cape fluttering.

"And get new tights! That's child abuse. We're gonna have nightmares!" Luke called.

"Nice one, dude," I said.

"That was helpful," Sophie said, sarcastically.

Just Charles looked down at his phone. His eyes bulged out of his head. "Guys! We have a hit on the security guard!"

"What does it say?" I asked. We all jostled for positioning to see his screen.

"They don't have a real name, but we have a screen name and location. HackerHoney? What the heck is that?"

"Well, C.T.'s worst nightmare just happened. A hacker stole his computer," I said.

"How do we find her before she does damage?" Cheryl asked.

"Anything on the crazy lady? Maybe if we find her, we find HackerHoney," Sophie said.

"Nope. Nothing. Bad photo plus a potential mask," Just Charles said.

"Can we search HackerHoney's friends list on Facebook or whatever old people use these days?" Luke asked.

"Good idea," Just Charles said. He typed in a whole bunch of stuff. After a few minutes, he said, "I don't know how to figure this out. We can't see anything. I'm not a member."

"There's Twitter," Sammie said. "Or Insta."

Just Charles opened his Twitter account. He searched for HackerHoney. She popped up. He scrolled through her profile and a bunch of tweets. Nothing that gave us any clue about her identity.

"See who she follows," I said.

Just Charles clicked on her follower list and scrolled down. "She follows C.T. And she follows Jimmy O'Beans. Coincidence?"

"But what do we do with that?" Sammie asked.

"Nothing," I said. "Dead end. Again."

CHAPTER 14

We sat around for a while, trying to figure out who Hacker-Honey was. Just Charles was, of course, slurping down more soda. I was watching closely to see if Evil Chuck was arriving any time soon, but he seemed okay so far. Perhaps all the walking around was burning the sugar off.

I got up to stretch my legs and saw Sergeant Villone. I turned around, not wanting him to see me. I didn't need him interfering with my investigation, but it didn't work.

From behind me, I heard Sergeant Villone say, "Staying out of trouble?"

"So far, so good," I said.

Ben walked up to us and said, "Did you tell him we questioned Grumpy Grimes?"

"You what?" Sergeant Villone shouted.

I wished Ben hadn't mentioned that. "We found and questioned the grumpy dude who disappeared," I said.

"You what? Stay out of this, I told you."

Ben gave me his best sheesh face and said, "Oops."

"C.T. asked me to help him," I said, defensively. "He told me he was counting on me."

Sergeant Villone shook his head. "He didn't say that to me. That's disappointing. Did he say anything about not trusting me?"

"No," I said, curiously. "So, where are you in the investigation?" I asked.

"Why are you so interested?" Sergeant Villone asked.

"I told you. I'm a fan of C.T.'s. He asked me to help. And I was involved in the actual robbery. Thor's hammer went up my butt."

Sergeant Villone stared down at me. "How were you involved?" he asked, accusatorially.

"I didn't mean from a criminal standpoint. I was at the scene."

"Why?"

"Taking a picture with Thor while waiting to get into C.T.'s panel discussion."

Ben added, "That Thor needs to stop eating so many burritos."

Sergeant Villone raised an eyebrow at Ben. "Anyway, so you're a fan."

"I already told you that," I said.

"You know, people who show too much interest in criminal investigations are often the perps trying to figure out how close the cops are to catching them."

"Interesting tidbit," I said, while Sergeant Villone stared at me, nearly salivating like I was a steak on his dinner plate. My heart was racing.

"You're young, geeky. You probably know computers. You may be the next evil tech genius for all I know."

"What? I had nothing to do with this," I said, defensively.

Sergeant Villone reached for his handcuffs. "That's a likely story. I'm gonna have to take you in for questioning."

I looked past Sergeant Villone like something dramatic was happening behind him. "Look! Spiderman's swinging on the ceiling!"

Sergeant Villone turned around and said, "Where?"

Ben followed, "Yeah, where?"

I grabbed Ben's arm and tugged. We ran as Sergeant Villone did a double take and found us making our getaway.

"Hey! I'm not finished with you!" Sergeant Villone said, running after us.

I looked over my shoulder and yelled to Ben, "Faster! We've gotta get out of here!" I called out to my crew, "Hey! Care to join us?"

My father's words of "Stay out of trouble," echoed in my brain. "Sorry, dad!" I yelled. I knew he couldn't hear me, but it helped ease my guilt a little bit.

Sergeant Villone was about twenty feet behind us, forcing his way through the crowd. I looked up ahead and I think my eyes bulged out of my head, but thankfully popped back into place. There were two cops about fifty feet ahead of us, both in football positions, seemingly ready to tackle us. I already had enough pileups for the day. I didn't need one that would result in my getting arrested.

I forgot to tell Sergeant Villone about the security guard's identity. but I wasn't gonna risk stopping, not when the potential for getting arrested was on the table. That would definitely land me in military school. My parents had threatened my brother and me with it for years. And we never even came close to getting arrested. This had boarding school written all over it.

I was running in slow motion. No, it wasn't for a cool effect. I just wasn't very athletic and couldn't run very fast. Thankfully, the cop was less than athletic himself, or at least was carrying a few extra pounds that kept him from maintaining a high rate of speed when chasing me.

If ever there was an environment I knew like the back of my hand, it was the super hero world. I had to use it to my advantage. I needed to create some mayhem. I looked around and I knew exactly how. I pointed to a crowd gathered off to the side of the hallway and yelled to a man dressed as Spiderman, "Spiderman, the Green Goblin!" I saw Cyclops/Scott Summers from X-Men and yelled, "Jean is kissing Wolverine!"

"Gross!" Cyclops yelled back.

"Well, aren't you going to do something about it?"

"I should, but whatever."

Uh oh. "Mystique! She's shape-shifted into the cop!"

He hopped up and looked directly at Sergeant Villone. I hoped he would try to tackle him, but the fake Cyclops just lifted up his sunglasses, attempting to fry the sergeant with his non-existent optic blast.

It was disappointing. Sergeant Villone ran past Cyclops with a furrowed brow and then continued the chase.

There were still two cops ahead of us that were going to be problematic unless I did something quickly. I yelled at the top of my lungs, "Avengers, assemble!"

We kept running toward the cops. My stomach began to churn. And then one of the great wonders of the world assembled right before our eyes: Avengers. Lots of them. And multiple versions of each character, each jostling for his rightful position in the crew. We ducked into the crowd and cut through. I could see the cops bobbing and weaving to try to find us, but there was too much commotion.

When we got to the end, I yelled, "Run for it!"

We all took off running, burst through the front doors, and out into the open air. We needed a game changer. I was running out of steam. Plus, with a smaller crowd outside, we had fewer obstacles to help us and the cop had an easier shot at communicating with other cops and security guards. And I knew Officer Fischer was gunning for me after the bomb disaster. I looked around at all the traffic, storefronts, buses, and cab lines, as I tried to keep up with Sophie and Luke.

And then I saw it. Our escape. What would become known as the Austinmobile. About a block away, there was a line of half a dozen pedicabs. You know, the bikes that transport a few people on a bench in the back.

"Our chariot awaits!" I yelled. "The pedicabs!"

Sophie led the way to the pedicabs. I turned around as we ran, to see Sergeant Villone still chasing us. I hoped the pedicab drivers would still want to take us somewhere after seeing a cop hot on our trail.

"Stop! I order you to halt!" Sergeant Villone yelled, while we all jumped into the pedicab seats.

"Go!" I yelled. "He's not a real cop! Just dressed like one for Comic Con to prey on unsuspecting children!"

The pedicab driver took off like a race car driver, his ponytail bouncing up and down as he peddled. Sophie and Luke were crammed in the pedicab with me. The rest of the crew was in a pedicab behind us. We jostled back and forth as the driver picked up speed and weaved around a couple jaywalking.

"That's illegal!" I yelled.

Luke yelled, "Follow that car!"

The pedicab driver turned around in the midst of his furious peddling. "What car?"

"I don't know. I just always wanted to say that. They always say that in the movies."

"Hold on!" the driver yelled.

I looked ahead to see a red stop light and ten or so cars stopped. We were going too fast to stop.

"Ahhh, farts!" I yelled.

Sophie looked out ahead. "I agree!"

"Me, too!" the driver yelled.

The trunk of the car ahead of us was rapidly approaching and we were actually speeding up.

"What are you doing?" Sophie yelled. "We're gonna die!"

CHAPTER 15

The pedicab driver didn't say a word, as we accelerated toward the trunk of the car ahead of us, heading for certain doom. A split second before we smashed into the car, he turned the handlebars, steering us toward the curb. The front tire surged up the handicap ramp, followed by the right tire of the back of our cab, but not the left. I grabbed Sophie by the arm in mid air, as we nearly bounced out of the pedicab.

People were diving left and right, as we were half on the sidewalk and half on the street, passing the cars stopped at the lights.

"Uh, oh," the driver said.

"What?" I yelled, and then I saw it. We had no room to get back onto the street and we were headed straight for a very thick and very sturdy-looking light pole.

The driver slammed on the brakes, which helped, but not much.

We all let out primal screams/shrieks as the pedicab slammed into the pole. The entire cab took flight and we almost flipped over. I grabbed onto what was closest. Unfortunately, it was Luke's butt, which actually helped quite a bit, because he grabbed something that kept us in the cab. The back wheels bounced when they hit the ground, the seat cracking in two. The three of us fell onto the sidewalk with a smack.

"The cop is coming!" Luke yelled.

"That'll be $8," the pedicab driver moaned, his ponytail busted and his hair strewn across his face, as he sat up against the pole.

"Thanks for the lift!" I yelled, as Sophie pulled me away.

Officer Villone was struggling, but we weren't doing that great ourselves. I think we were putting distance between us and him, but then things got worse. I heard sirens from a distance and then saw a police car spin around the corner. It screeched to a stop, people scattering all around. The doors popped open, expelling two police officers.

I didn't know what to do. Things had gotten out of hand, quickly. I was public enemy number one. Police cars were showing up to try to capture me. I saw a bunch of Star Wars enthusiasts, dressed in various costumes, and playing with remote-controlled R2-D2 and BB-8 droids.

I yelled, "Help me, Obi-Wan. You're our only hope!"

A black-bearded Ben Kenobi stepped forward, his eyes wide.

"Imperial guards!" I added.

Ben Kenobi grabbed a controller from a five-foot Chewbacca, commandeering the control of R2-D2. With precision, Ben steered R2-D2 into the path of the two police officers/imperial guards, who were running in single file. The first officer spotted the droid too late, attempted to hop over it, but ended up stumbling over it instead. He fell to the ground. His partner quickly followed. R2-D2 sputtered out of control. Smoke sizzled out of its top. The pint-sized Chewbacca roared at the status of his toy/droid.

We continued running and ended up cutting down a side street that had a lot of hiding places. Nobody was following us. I pointed to a sign above a store front that read, "Francesco's Pizzeria" and yelled, "In there!" We slowed to a stop, tore the door open, and huddled inside. The crowd was pretty large. We pushed inside to avoid being seen from the outside.

Sophie was scanning the sidewalk outside and said, "Nobody's coming. We're safe."

"What...happened?" Sammie asked, gasping for air.

"The cop was going to arrest me...Take me in for questioning."

"Why did you run?" Sophie asked.

"I didn't do anything wrong," I said, defensively.

"This is bad," Cheryl said. "You should turn yourself in."

"He didn't have a warrant for my arrest. He was making things up as he went along. We solve the case, as planned. Nothing's changed."

"What now?" Ben asked.

"Let's grab some pizza and come up with a plan," I said.

Luke said, "It's not Frank's, but Francesco's can't be too far off."

Darth Faker didn't seem to think so. The costumed man a few feet ahead of us stood at the counter, complaining. "This is burnt," he said in a deep voice.

"You get what you get. Unless you want to wait another ten minutes," the old dude, Vinny, said from behind the counter.

Darth Vader held up his hand, attempting to use the Force to choke Vinny. For some reason, it didn't appear to be working. Vinny smirked as Darth's hand shook, seemingly using every ounce of strength he had to choke Vinny from two feet away without touching him.

"Are you finished?" Vinny asked, annoyed.

Apparently, Darth was not. He said, "Give into your hate and anger. Turn to the Dark Side!"

Vinny looked around Darth Vader and said, "Next!"

Darth dropped his hand in disappointment, grabbed his burnt pizza slice, and slumped over to the seating area.

We ordered two pies and sodas, and then sat down. Even though it was after lunch time, it was a mad house. Half the Guardians of the Galaxy were there and Vader had assembled six Storm Troopers. There were a bunch of other random caped crusaders scattered around as well. Luke, Just Charles, and Cheryl sat across from the rest of us.

Just Charles was scanning Instragram posts by HackerHoney.

"Any luck?" I asked.

"Nothing yet," he said. "So, we're safe for now, but how are we gonna get back into the show if the cops are looking for Austin?" Just Charles asked.

"They're not the best cops I've ever seen," I said. "They probably don't even know who I am. Plus, we have armed guards." I nodded to the Storm Troopers.

Ben countered, "Yeah, but we're part of the rebellion. The Storm Troopers aren't going to protect us."

"Don't tell them that," I said.

"Who wants to be a Storm Trooper anyway?" Luke said.

"I know," Sophie said. "They're so dumb and they have terrible training."

That folks, was just one of the few reasons I was crazy about her.

"They can't shoot a laser to save their lives. Literally," Ben said.

"You would think Darth Vader would've trained them better. He doesn't seem to be one who tolerates stupidity," I said. "But we can debate Vader's employee development shortcomings when we get home. We have to figure out this mystery."

Luke, Just Charles, and Cheryl looked up and froze. Luke dropped his pizza. Just Charles looked like he might cry.

I wasn't sure I wanted to turn around, but before I could, I heard a deep voice behind me. "You dare to disrespect the Dark Lord?"

I turned around to see Darth Vader towering above me. I stuttered and stammered, not sure what to say.

A chair squeaked as someone stood up abruptly. I turned to see none other than the most-evil wizard ever to walk the earth, Harry Potter's nemesis, Voldemort! Well, he kinda looked like him. He didn't have the strange nose/gill thing going, but still, his costume and makeup were pretty close. He pointed his wand at Darth Vader and asked, "Who's disrespecting me?"

"Nobody's talking about you," Darth Vader said, annoyed. "Sit down and eat your pumpkin pizza or whatever it is you eat."

"I'm the Dark Lord!" Voldemort shrieked.

"Are not," Darth Vader said.

"Am too."

"Are not."

And then they both shouted together, "I'm the Dark Lord!"

The entire restaurant sat there in stunned silence, nobody seemingly sure of what to do, as the evil Dark Lords disagreed.

Darth Vader blurted out, "Jinx!"

"That's not fair! I can never win the Jinx game! Nobody dares speak my name!"

"Doesn't matter," Darth Vader said, giddy. "You lose! I'm the rightful Dark Lord!"

A bunch of people cheered.

Voldy scanned the room with his wand. The cheering people shut up quickly.

Darth Vader looked at me and said, "This isn't finished, young Jedi." He threw his cape over his shoulder with pizzazz and walked away, his Storm Troopers on his heels. He sat back down at his table across the room and lifted up his mask to take a bite of pizza.

Voldy collapsed into his chair and angry-ate his garlic knots. He tore bites off with his teeth like a rabid dog, in between muttering to himself. The guy seated across from him, dressed as Draco Malfoy, scooted his chair back.

I looked at the crew. "We have bigger problems. C.T.'s

laptop is still missing and the cops are after me because they think I'm now the number one suspect."

"So, now what do we do?" Sophie asked.

Just Charles raised his fists in the air, almost punching a zombie in the face. "We got her!"

"What do you mean?" I asked.

Just Charles held out his phone for us all to see. "Look at this post. It has her signature."

"I can't read script," Luke said. "What good is that?"

"It says her name is Elvira Elmwood. This is it!" Sophie yelled.

"Now we know who the security guard is. Check the white pages. See if she lives locally," I said.

Cheryl pulled out her phone and started searching. "Nothing," she said.

"So, if she doesn't live locally, she must be staying nearby," Ben said.

"It could be with a friend. Or in a hotel. What if it's an alias?" Sophie asked.

I said, "We've gotta try. Find a list of nearby hotels. Everybody call one and ask to be connected to her. Then hang up before she connects you. Let's call hotels until we find where she's staying."

Sammie pulled up a list of local hotels on Google Maps and we dialed number after number. I lost count of how many we called.

"Guys," Luke said, glumly. "What if she's staying at a Holiday Inn Express? According to the commercials, don't they make you smarter? She could have the brain of Megamind or something."

"Dude, I think you need to stay at a Holiday Inn Express," I said, to laughter.

We kept dialing. There were only a few hotels left near

the convention center that we hadn't called. If we had to increase the search radius, we would be calling hotels all day.

I dialed another number. I nearly fell asleep as the phone rang. A woman picked up. "Front desk. The Garden Inn. How may I help you?"

"Yes, hi. Can you connect me to Elvira Elmwood?"

I heard typing on the other end. "One moment, please," the woman said, cheerily.

I hung up the phone. "Guys! I found her."

Sammie zoomed out on her map app.

I pointed to the hotel on the map. "It's there."

"It's only three blocks away," Cheryl said.

"Let's go!" I yelled. "We've got a lead."

We all jumped up, reenergized. As I turned to leave, I bumped into someone. I looked up, fear surging through my body.

CHAPTER 16

The fully-nosed Voldemort stared down at me and whispered, "We meet again for the last time."

"Isn't that a Toy Story line?" I asked.

"Maybe," he said, defensively. "Is the Dark Lord unable to enjoy the cinema? I should've finished you off when we first met." The faux Voldemort pulled out his wand and pointed it in my face.

The crowd cheered, as someone pushed their way toward me. A man wearing wizard robes, glasses, and a scruffy beard stepped in front of me, nearly nose to nose with Voldy.

The hairy Harry Potter said, "You'll put your wand away if you know what's good for you." He lifted his hair, revealing a lightning bolt-shaped scar, albeit on the wrong side and half smeared from sweat, but it didn't detract from the tension.

"Or if you prefer," Harry said, showing the inside of his robes and revealing his own wand.

Some people cleared out of the room, while others just took a few steps back to give the two wizards some space to duel. It was the courteous thing to do.

The two powerful wizards circled each other, their wands at the ready.

Sophie tugged on my arm and said, "We gotta go."

"The duel is my favorite part from the books. They totally botched it in the movies," I said, not moving.

"This is more important," Sophie said, tugging harder.

"Ugh. Okay," I said, following her.

As we exited the room, Voldemort yelled, "Get him!"

I looked over my shoulder to see six Storm Troopers take off running toward us, knocking over chairs and bumping tables, like the uncoordinated buffoons that they are.

Darth Vader slammed down his pizza and yelled, "Idiots!"

Hairy Harry yelled, "Expelliarmus!" as Voldy yelled, "Avada Kedavra!"

"Thanks, Harry, gotta go!" I yelled, as we ran out of Francesco's and into the street.

"What now?" Ben asked, nearly falling over a girl dressed as Dora the Explorer.

"Lo siento!" I yelled, which is 'I'm sorry' in Spanish. Señora Fuentes, my Spanish teacher, would've been proud.

"Anybody have an invisibility cloak?" Just Charles asked.

We weaved in and out of small pockets of people and parked cars that lined the street, the Storm Troopers still hot on our trail. Yes, they were uncoordinated buffoons, but we were uncoordinated nerds. There wasn't much difference when it came to athletic prowess.

"Let's find a cargo hold!" I screamed.

"What are you talking about?" Sammie yelled back.

"Star Wars! The Millennium Falcon! Han Solo was a smuggler! He had a secret cargo hold!" I yelled, like she was the dumbest person in the world, which wasn't true, but it sure felt like it at that moment.

"Yeah, because there are secret cargo holds everywhere!" Sammie yelled.

She made a good point. The rhythmic clopping of the Storm Troopers boots on the pavement was growing louder. I turned back to see them only forty or fifty feet away.

"Around the corner!" I yelled to Sophie and Luke, who were ahead of me. Ben and Sammie were on each side of me, while Just Charles was lagging behind, Cheryl pulling him by his arm.

"Hey, Soph!" I yelled through gasps. "Is it a bad time to toss out a Halloween costume idea?"

"Of course not," she said, sarcastically. "I'm actually kinda bored right now."

"I'm thinking I go as Han Solo and you as Princess Leia?"

"I do like the idea of being a princess and the Cinnabon hair. But what happened to Harry and Ginny?"

"Let's do both."

"Can we get out of this jam first?" Ben yelled, annoyed. I think he was upset that he hadn't called dibs on the idea yet.

We made another turn down a deserted side street, the Storm Troopers out of view.

There was a bunch of industrial-sized garbage bins lining the street.

Ben looked over at me as we ran. "Are you thinking what I'm thinking?"

"Yep. We got the wrong Star Wars hiding spot. Unfortunately," I said, gasping. "Everybody, into a garbage bin!" I yelled, recalling the scene from the movie where they blast their way into a disgusting garbage disposal. I only hoped there wouldn't be any creatures looking to kill us in these bins.

"Really?" Sammie asked.

"Yes!"

Sophie and Luke already disappeared into a bin. Just Charles and Cheryl dove behind another. I ran up to a garbage bin that had its lid open. It was about chest high. I was going full out. Mr. Muscalini would've been proud. I jumped, grabbed the edge of the metal bin, and pulled. Nothing happened. I threw in a few grunts, hoping they would help lift my feet, but it was useless. I kinda just hung there, while Ben helped Sammie into a bin and then climbed in. I continued to struggle, but then heard the clopping of boots growing stronger. They were around the corner now and heading toward us. I only hoped they hadn't seen me yet. I let go of the bin and ran around the side, scrambling to find a hiding spot among a bunch of cardboard boxes and shipping pallets.

I closed my eyes, as if that would help my stealthiness. I heard wheezing coming from inside the garbage bin. I couldn't control my own breath, either. I was sucking in massive amounts of air, attempting to catch my nerdy breath. And I wasn't doing a great job of it.

The footsteps stopped, which wasn't a good sign. I had hoped they would pass right by. I tried hard to listen to their whereabouts, but I couldn't hear anything above my own breathing. I contemplated opening my eyes, but didn't.

Instead, I heard the voice of Darth Vader say, "I've been looking forward to this moment for some time. Your friends can join us from the garbage as well. This is Star Wars, not Garbage Pail Kids."

I opened my eyes to see two rows of three Storm Troopers lined up in front of me and Darth Vader to their left. They were all looking at me through the slits in the shipping pallets.

"Garbage Pail Kids? I don't even know what that means," I said. I stood up and walked out into the street.

My friends emerged from behind and inside the garbage bins.

"Glad we did that," Sophie said, shaking her head.

Darth looked at me and said, "It's time you embrace the dark side. The force is strong with you."

"Never!" I yelled.

"Then we fight to the death," he said, darkly. Darth Faker pulled out his light saber and pressed the button. Nothing happened. "Come on, really?" He whacked it with his other hand and pressed the button again. "This is so embarrassing." He pressed the button repeatedly, growing more and more frustrated each time, but the red luminescent plasma blade remained stubbornly inside the crystal chamber. "Dang it!" he yelled, stomping his giant, black boot on the ground.

A Storm Trooper walked over to the garbage bin with my friends, bent down, and returned with an adjustable shower rod. "How about this, my lord?" he said, holding the rod like a sword.

The lousy Lord Vader took the shower rod from the Storm Trooper and said, surprised, "Look at you, FN-2123. Using your brain." Darth pulled the adjustable curtain rod apart, separating it into two pieces. He tossed one to me.

The rod soared through the air to me. I stepped forward and reached for the rod, which was falling perfectly horizontally in front of me. I closed my grip, too soon, of course. The rod hit my knuckles and clanked to the ground.

"Oops," I said. I leaned down to pick it up.

"The force with this one is not as strong as I once thought," Darth Vader said, disappointed.

"This is pathetic," one of the Storm Troopers said.

"Zip it, FN-2245! I'm the only one who can criticize my son!"

"What is going on?" Sammie whispered to Ben.

"He thinks Austin is Luke Skywalker."

"This is getting a little too crazy," I said, gripping the shower rod with both hands.

"Sorry you had to find out that way, son," Darth said. "But they're not Storm Troopers for their brains."

"That's rude," Sophie said.

Darth stepped toward Sophie with his shower rod sword.

I darted forward and met his blade with mine, before he could get any closer to Sophie. I was the best equipped to battle with the faux Darth Vader via light saber/curtain rod. I had once trained to become a knight on a medieval quest. Perhaps you remember that adventure. I tried to remember my training. Circles and bubbles. Don't let Vader into my circle. Pop the bubbles. I was referring to my training where I thrust my sword/hockey stick at the unstoppable horde of bubbles from an old bubble machine.

Vader turned to me, brandishing his sword in my direction.

I got into my best sword fighting stance, holding the saber with both hands to the side of my head, while Vader held his saber straight out in front of him with both hands.

"Your friends may escape, but you are doomed." He surged forward, his sword behind his head, and unleashed a massive blow.

CHAPTER 17

The faux Vader surged toward me, his sword slicing through the air toward my head. I stepped to the side and parried the blow. Before I could counter his attack, Vader unleashed a fury of blows that I barely was able to block, parry, and dodge. My epic battle with Randy flooded my mind. Vader was stronger than Randy, but not as quick. I moved my feet as fast as I could to evade Vader's attacks, deftly stepping out of his circle, time and time again. Until, well, I didn't. Vader sliced an overhead attack toward me. I jumped into the air, attempting to dodge the attack, but it clanked down, hitting my sword and then my shoulder. Pain surged through my body, as I stumbled forward.

I was on one knee, holding my sword with one hand, as Vader's sword sliced through the air once more. It connected with my hand. My light saber flew from my hand and tumbled to the ground. It rolled to a stop at Sophie's feet.

I held my hand in pain, still down on one knee.

Sophie screamed, "No!"

"I am your father. It is useless to resist," Vader said. He

lifted his mask a touch and said, "Man, it's sweaty in this mask," to no one in particular.

"No!" I yelled.

Sophie picked up my saber and tossed it to me, as I stood up. The light saber soared in my direction yet again. My fingers collapsed around the rusty rod. Energy surged through my body.

"I did it," I said, surprised. "I did it!"

My crew cheered.

"Great job, son!" Faux Vader yelled.

I surged forward, attempting to catch Doofus Darth in a moment of fatherly weakness, but sadly, I did not. He blocked my vicious attack. He stepped back, as we both regrouped, ready to battle once more.

I took a deep breath and re-centered, remembering my

training. I felt like a new man, or at least a new boy. Calm, but strong.

We closed the space between us with yet another clanking blow above our heads.

"Obi-wan has taught you well."

I pulled my light saber back, as I was going to wind up for a devastating overhead smash, but I stopped halfway and brought my round blade down sharply toward the evil Jedi's hands, surprising him. My blade connected with his gloved hands. His own light saber fell from his clutches, clanked onto the ground, and rolled away, disappearing underneath the garbage dumpster.

Vader dropped to one knee and held his hand in pain. "Oww, it hurts so bad," Vader said, sniffling.

"Are you crying?" one of the Storm Troopers asked. He looked at the other Storm Troopers. "Is he crying?"

"No! I'm not crying."

"He's totally crying," the Storm Trooper said in disbelief, shaking his head.

Vader looked up at the inquiring Storm Trooper. "It really hurts! I didn't see any of you take a savage blow to an appendage!" Darth took off his helmet, revealing a way too old man. He dropped his helmet on the ground and bowed his head to me. "I yield to you, master. Forgive me for my digression to the dark side."

I looked around at my relieved crew. I wiped the sweat from my brow and said, "All is forgiven, guys. It's been fun and all, but we really have to go."

The Storm Troopers stepped to the side and stood at attention.

"Until we meet again in a galaxy far, far away," Ben said, as we hustled past them.

"I love you, son!" Vader yelled out. "Don't forget to visit your old man sometimes!"

CHAPTER 18

We ran out of the alley, following Sammie and her Google Maps app. We made a few turns and quickly found the Garden Inn. We entered the hotel. It was bustling with activity. It looked like a wedding between Marvel and DC Comics. There were people dressed as movie characters everywhere.

"We need to get a room number," Sophie said.

"Shouldn't be a problem," I said. "Let me do it. I think if we're all together, they might get suspicious."

"Okay," she said, heading over to the rest of the crew.

I joined the short line at the hotel's front desk. I craned around some dude dressed as Thanos, but obviously not as big as the oversized Avenger's villain, to see a faux Aquaman standing at the front desk with Green Lantern, talking to the woman behind the counter.

"The pool is pathetic," the Aquaman wannabe said. "The chlorine levels are off the charts. It's just not natural."

The Green Lantern cut in. "Who cares about the pool? Have you found a ring? I'm useless without it."

"Real men don't wear rings," Aquaman said.

"Yeah, they do. Wedding rings," Green Lantern said, annoyed.

"Did you lose your wedding ring?"

"No," Green Lantern said, hanging his head. "It's my Power ring." He looked up and pleaded with the woman behind the desk. "Please, I need it. It completes me. His mane of hair will survive a little too much chlorine."

"Really, dude?" Aquaman asked, angrily. "You want me to go get my trident?"

The woman cut in. "We will check the chlorine levels in the pool, sir. We haven't had anyone turn in a ring, Power or otherwise, but if you give me your name, I'll reach out to you if we find it."

"The name's Green Lantern," the man said, charmingly.

The woman rolled her eyes. She pushed a piece of paper in front of him and said, "Write down your phone number, Mr. Lantern."

I finally made it to the front of the line. The woman looked over the counter at me. "Can I help you?" she asked.

"Yes," I said, softly. "I feel really stupid, but I forgot what room I'm in with my mom, Elvira Elmwood."

"Of course, don't worry about it." The woman typed into the computer and looked back up at me. "I can't give you a key, but it's room 322."

"I went to 222," I said, shaking my head. "The Green Goblin was not amused."

"He never is," she said. "Have a good day."

"Thanks," I said, with a wave.

I walked back over to my crew. They were lined up against the wall next to the elevators, which was kind of fitting, since I could've ended up in a police lineup. And still could have, I guess.

"So, now what?" Cheryl asked. "We know where they're at, but what are we gonna do with that info?"

"Yeah, we're not the cops," Just Charles.

"We can't bust down the door like a S.W.A.T. team," Luke said, and then continued, excitedly, "Or can we?"

"That would be totally awesome," Ben said.

"Do you have a battering ram in your backpack?" Luke asked me.

I shook my head, not knowing how to even answer the question.

"Dang it!" Luke yelled. "What about you, Ben?"

"Left it at home."

"Ugh. So disappointing," Luke said.

"Should we call them?" Sophie asked. "Pretend to be room service?"

"Or housekeeping," Sammie added. "Everybody needs more towels."

"What do we do then?" I asked.

Nobody had any answers.

"A battering ram is the answer," Luke muttered.

My phone dinged. It was Kyle asking where we were. I texted him, 'Garden Inn. Hot on the laptop trail.' I looked up and said, "Why don't we just go and have a look around up there?" I asked.

"What if they see us?" Just Charles asked.

"Let's just have a peek and see. We're just kids walking down the hallway. They don't know we're looking for them. They have no idea we're coming for them."

We took the elevator to the third floor and then found the room. The seven of us stood outside of it, like a bunch of idiots, not sure what to do. I put my ear to the door. Sophie joined me. I heard voices inside, but I couldn't make out what they were saying.

"I want to listen," Luke said, like a five-year old.

"Shhh," I whispered. "I can't hear what they're saying."

"What do you hear?" Just Charles whispered.

"I hear you asking questions," I whispered, angrily.

"Maybe we should rent the room above this one and climb down from the balcony," Luke offered.

"Are you nuts?" Ben asked.

"What?" Luke asked, defensively. "We could use suction cups or something."

"Yeah, I'd trust suction cups on the side of a building three stories up," Ben said, shaking his head.

I couldn't hear anything with all the bickering. I lay down on the floor and put my ear to the crack under the door. I could hear their conversation much more clearly.

I relayed what I had heard. "They were talking about cracking the password. This is it, guys! We've got 'em!"

"Shhh," Sophie said.

"What are we going to do now?" Sammie asked.

"Let's call the police. This isn't for us to solve," Cheryl said.

"We should've brought Vader and the Storm Troopers," Ben said.

"That Vader didn't even know how to use the force. I mean, honestly," Just Charles said.

A door opened behind us, revealing an oversized dude carrying a bucket of ice and Thor's hammer. It wasn't immediately clear if it was the same Thor's hammer that was up my butt or not. Everyone stepped to the side and pretended like we were waiting for someone.

"Just act natural," I whispered, as if lying on the floor in the hallway of a hotel was natural. "I'm sure he's just passing through."

The man furrowed his brow as he looked down at us.

"Hello, sir," Sophie said. "Enjoying the convention?"

He ignored Sophie's question. He nodded to me. "What are you doing?"

"I'm a nerd, sir. I fell over. It happens 22.6% of the time."

"And what did you mean when you said, 'We got 'em!'?"

I got up to my feet, thinking. "Umm, I crushed a bug when I fell."

"And the part about the police?"

"It was on the Federal Bug Investigation's Most Wanted list," I said.

To add more excitement before we got smashed by a giant with Thor's hammer, the door to room 322 opened, revealing the security guard. Her hair was down to her shoulders without the hat and she was in jeans and a t-shirt, but it was definitely Elvira Elmwood, the security guard from the scene of the stolen laptop.

"What's going on out here?"

The hammer man said, "I found this crew snooping around."

I looked around. It would be hard to get past the dude and back to the elevator, but there were stairs behind us. I wasn't convinced we would all make it. Before I could say anything, Elvira nodded and the giant held out his arm and swept us into the room, like an enormous bowling lane sweeper. We smashed into each other, attempting to stay upright, but ultimately ended in a heap of elbows and knees.

"What are you doing?" Cheryl yelled at Elvira.

"Get 'em in here and we'll figure this out," Elvira said.

"Move," the giant dude said, pushing us forward.

We had to get out of there. It wasn't going to end well. I was going to make a run for the door. Somebody had to escape to alert the police. I took a deep breath, did a spin move, and rushed for the door. "Run!" I yelled.

The giant reached for me, as I spun around his hip. He gripped my shirt and tossed me back into the room toward the others. I collided with Just Charles, who stumbled back and knocked a lamp, which hit the ice bucket, which crashed to the floor, and spread the ice in every direction.

"Who's gonna pay for that?" Elvira asked.

"Him," the giant said, pointing at me. "With his life." He looked at me and smiled. "Just kidding. Maybe. It depends on what the boss tells me to do."

"And she's the boss?" Sophie asked, pointing at the guard.

"Nope. The boss will be here any minute."

I whispered to Sophie. "Do you think the boss is the crazy lady?"

She nodded.

The guard looked at the giant henchman and said, "Why did you have to steal Thor's hammer?"

"It's super cool. You stole a laptop."

Elvira rolled her eyes. "We don't need the God of Thunder coming here looking for his hammer."

"Can't he just summon it?" Just Charles asked.

"I don't know," Elvira answered, annoyed. She looked at the henchman and asked, "Really, why did you do that?"

"It's Thor's hammer," he said, defensively. "It even smells good." He held the hammer to his nose and sniffed a big, crazy sniff.

"That was in Austin's butt," Ben said.

"That's private," I whispered, angrily.

"Oh, sorry."

"Welcome," Elvira said. "Please have a seat and take out your phones. Kids are too attached to their devices these days."

I sat down in between Sophie and Luke on a couch in the corner of the suite. The security guard moved a few chairs from the kitchenette's table for the rest of the crew to sit down.

Sophie slipped her hand down between us, pushing something in between the couch cushions.

The henchman walked toward the couch, holding out a laundry bag. "Phones in here," he said, gruffly.

I reached up, about to place mine in the bag, as did Luke. I forced out a giant, fake sneeze. And totally failed to cover. I sprayed spit all over the henchman. He turned away to shield himself from the snot attack. I quickly put my phone in the bag with Luke. Sophie held her empty hand up to the bag as well, pretending to drop something into the bag. I hoped the henchman had been distracted enough to not realize only two phones had been dropped in.

"Sorry," I said, sheepishly.

The henchman shook his head, as he turned to Cheryl sitting on the chair. I was pretty certain he bought our illusion. That is, until he frowned, looked into the bag and said, "Wait a second. There are only two in here. Where's the other one?"

Sophie looked at me in a panic. I tried to play it cooler by keeping my facial expressions nondescript, but still peeing in my pants. In the past, I'd been known to wear a diaper from time to time. This was not one of those times. The room was a tad chilly, so at least I was a bit warmer for a few minutes.

The henchman took out two phones and placed them on the coffee table at my knees. "Whose phone is missing?"

"We're a couple, so we use the same phone," I said, pointing to Sophie.

"You're not a couple," the henchman said, laughing.

"We are!" I yelled, angrily.

The henchman looked at Sophie for answers. "It's true," she said.

Again, I thought he would buy it, but he didn't. "Stand up."

I looked at Sophie. There was nothing we could do. He would toss us around like a rag doll if we didn't do as we were told.

"I don't have a phone," I said. "Really."

"What kid doesn't have a phone these days?"

"Plenty of kids," I said.

"I don't believe you. Give it to me or when I find it, I will crush it with Thor's hammer."

Sophie's eyes bulged. She reached into the couch and revealed her phone. "Must've fallen out of my pocket," she said, sheepishly.

"You don't have pockets," Luke added, unhelpfully.

The henchman said, "Sit down. And don't play with me. I bite."

The rest of the crew offered their phones with no funny business. My mind raced, trying to figure out what we could do to escape or at least signal someone about our captivity.

The henchman disappeared into the bedroom with a bag of phones and returned without them.

"Our parents are going to be looking for us," Just Charles said. "Don't do anything stupid."

"Thanks for the reminder," Elvira said. She looked over at the henchman and said, "Remove the batteries and SIM cards."

I slumped back in my seat.

Just Charles whispered, "Oops."

The henchman returned, walking straight toward the kitchen table and Thor's hammer. He picked it up and searched the kitchen until he spotted an empty soda can. His face lit up. He placed the soda can on the table in front of him and lined up the hammer's path to connect with the top of the can. He pulled the hammer back over his head and grunted, dropping the hammer to the table.

The can bent with a creak, but the blow didn't crush it entirely. Still, it was pretty good for a semi-toy hammer.

"This thing stinks," the henchman said, tossing the hammer onto the table.

"You don't know the half of it," I said.

"What does that mean?" the henchman asked.

"Shut up. Don't talk to them," Elvira said, sternly.

"Before you play with your toys, do you mind taping them up?"

"Okay," the henchman said, moping into the other room.

I stood up and yelled again, "Run!" I set my sights on the security guard who stood between me and the door. Our best chance to escape was when the henchman was in the other room, unable to stop us. I pushed off the ground in an effort to hurdle the coffee table that stood at my knees. I did not accomplish what I had set out to do. My shin banged the side of the table. I yelped, as I toppled over the table and onto the floor.

Bodies, screams, a broken coffee table, and toppling chairs mixed into one giant mess of a recipe. I got up to my knees, but Luke tumbled over me, both of us falling to the ground. Thankfully, I didn't fart. I was too busy kissing the seemingly never-before cleaned carpet.

"Get off of me," I said.

Sophie grabbed my arm and pulled me up. I looked toward the door. Ben, Cheryl, Just Charles, and Sammie were grappling with Elvira, who was blocking the hallway, trying to keep them all contained.

The henchman returned, nearly ripping the door off its hinges in the process, and quickly returned the room to order. He grabbed Ben and Just Charles, one in each hand, and tossed them toward the chairs. The security guard wrapped her arms around Sammie and forced her back toward the chairs as well, while the henchman easily moved Cheryl back.

Sophie, Luke, and I looked at how easily the rest of the crew had been returned to captivity and just decided to sit back down.

"Sorry about the coffee table," I said. "You can charge it to the room."

"Funny," Elvira said. "I don't have time for this. We still have to take care of the laptop and he's coming back soon. He's not gonna be happy."

"Who's *he*?" I asked.

"None of your business," Elvira growled.

A buzzing echoed from the front door. Elvira's face dropped. The door swung open.

"Honey I'm home!" a voice called out, and then, "What the heck?"

The voice sounded familiar, but I couldn't place it. We would find out soon enough. The man entered the room. He wore a hat pulled down so low that I couldn't see his face. He took off the hat and looked at all of us. It was Jimmy O'Beans!

"Who the heck are these clowns? What's going on here?" Jimmy asked.

Sophie yelled, "This is kidnapping!"

"Are you sure you want to go down this path?" Cheryl added.

Jimmy shrugged. "Yep. We might go farther."

"What does that mean?" I asked, my voice shaking.

"I don't know. It just sounded good. It was scary, right?"

"Definitely."

"You should be terrified," Jimmy said. "Can somebody tell me why they're here and why we're adding kidnapping to the mix?"

"Come on, Jimmy. You're a children's author. This isn't you," Cheryl said.

"Okay, shut them up. They're already annoying me. Grab the duct tape." Jimmy nodded to the henchman and then to the tape on the floor.

"Ah, really?" I asked.

"What? Duct tape is awesome," Jimmy said.

"It almost got me expelled last year," I said. "I just don't like the stuff."

"Get an extra-large piece for this one's mouth," Jimmy said, pointing to me.

The henchman stepped toward me, the coffee table crunching under his heavy foot. He tore a piece of tape off with ease.

"Do you have to do that?" I asked. "I've been trying to grow in my mustache," I said.

"Where?" the henchman asked.

"That's hurtful," I said.

The henchman placed the tape over my mouth and then lined up a piece for Luke.

"I'm good, du-," Luke said. He got a piece anyway in mid-sentence.

Sophie chimed in. "Do you have a name or should we just call you evil henchman?"

He didn't answer. He just taped up her beautiful face.

Jimmy looked at Elvira. "Why are they here?" he asked, annoyed.

"They were snooping around outside the room. They tracked us here. They know about the laptop. They were at the scene."

"This is wonderful. Excellent work," Jimmy said, sarcastically. He gave a thumbs up and a forced smile for good measure.

"Thanks, boss," the henchman answered, apparently not sensing the sarcasm.

"How is he involved in this?" Cheryl whispered to us.

I shrugged.

The rest of the crew was taped up. It was the first time in a long time our crew was silent for more than a few minutes. Usually, somebody had something to say. And we still did.

We just couldn't say anything other than, "Shmirfenstuven-haven." So, of course, Cheryl Van Snoogle-Something kept thinking we were calling her when we were really trying to escape.

"Where are we on cracking the password?" Jimmy nodded over to the laptop that sat on the desk off to the side of the room. A small device was attached to the laptop that looked like a digital clock, except that there were too many numbers and letters, and the time changed too fast. So, not really like a clock at all.

"The fingerprint from the water bottle didn't work, so we have to crack it the hard way. It's only a matter of time. It's running every possible password combination."

"We're running out of time. The press release is less than an hour away!" Jimmy said. He looked at us and said, "Let's head into the other room to finish this discussion." He led the way into the side room and closed the door.

I used my supersonic hearing to pick up what they were saying. We were all leaning as close to the door as we could, even though we were all at least ten feet away.

"What are we supposed to do now? These kids know who we are. What else do they know?" Jimmy asked.

"They know we stole the laptop and plan on crashing the press conference. Perhaps you shouldn't have said anything in front of them," Elvira said.

"Perhaps you shouldn't have tied them up in our room without asking," Jimmy spat back.

"Had I asked, would you have let me?"

"I don't know," Jimmy said, annoyed. "I'm going to have a little discussion with them. You put us in a real bad spot."

"Sorry, Jimmy."

The door opened. Jimmy came out while the other two remained inside the bedroom. He looked at us and said,

"We need to have a little conversation. I need to know what you know. And I need to know now." He waited for a moment and said, "I'm waiting."

We all looked at each other's duct taped mouths and then struggled to talk.

I said, "Horfenfarfaloof!"

Sophie said, "Merfel, merfel, merfel."

Luke said, "I want my mommy!" Apparently, his tape job was faulty. The henchman hadn't waited until Luke stopped talking before putting the tape on originally. Luke's face flushed red.

"What? I can't understand any of you. Except you," he said, pointing at Luke. "Your mommy ain't coming." Jimmy walked over to Just Charles and tore off the tape.

"Owww!"

"I will ask again. What do you know?"

"Nothing?" Just Charles answered.

"We both know that ain't true," Jimmy said, smirking.

"Well, if we never say anything, it's like we know nothing."

"Hmm. You were in the front row of my panel discussion, were you not? I know that I was not given any front row seats for my fans," he said, bitterly. "And neither was the illustrator, so you were guests of one Chadwick Theloneus Walsh."

"That's not his real name," Just Charles said.

"It is if I say it is," Jimmy said, harshly.

"Okay, we'll give you that one," Just Charles said, shrugging.

"And if you were his guests, you must be loyal fans. Therefore, I can't trust you won't say anything."

"You could turn yourself in before you get in a lot of

trouble. First theft, now kidnapping. Who knows what other crimes you committed?" Just Charles asked.

The henchman peeked out from the bedroom, listening.

Just Charles pointed to him and said, "He stole Thor's hammer. He's the God of Thunder. That's a serious matter."

"He's kinda right, boss," the henchman said.

"Shut your dumb face, Bert!"

"Your name is Bert?" Just Charles asked.

"Maybe. What's it to you?"

"It just doesn't seem to fit that well."

"It doesn't, does it?"

"Marma herma rummer," I said.

"Huh?" Jimmy said. He walked over to me and tore the duct tape off my mouth.

"Owww! My mustache, dude!" I yelled. I looked at Bert and said, "I think your name should be tougher. Something like Skull Crusher."

"That's pretty cool," Bert said. "I was thinking of Raul. How does that-"

"Knock it off! All of you! Tape them back up!" Jimmy shook his head. "This is turning into a big mistake. I should just flush this all down the toilet. That's where terrible potty jokes belong."

"I don't think the laptop is gonna flush," I said.

"It's a good point."

Bert taped my mouth up again. It was fun while it lasted. At least I got to give out a cool nickname. I just hoped he wouldn't live up to it while we were still there.

Elvira came out to check on the laptop.

Jimmy said to her, "We have to continue on the timeline. I've gotta go change."

"No, please stay the wonderful person you are," Bert said.

"Idiot." Jimmy left the room, shaking his head.

Jimmy returned about twenty minutes later. At least we assumed it was Jimmy. He looked more like C.T. than Jimmy, so he was much more handsome. He was wearing a baseball hat and a light turtleneck. I took a close look and it seemed like Jimmy was wearing a mask of C.T. It was super high quality. And then it hit me. The piece of rubber on the wig. Jimmy was the crazy lady!

"Smurfledarfenludenheim." I said.

"What?" Jimmy asked, annoyed. He walked over to me and tore off the duct tape again.

"Owww!" I yelled. I didn't want to say anything about the crazy lady, so I bluffed. "You look just like him. That's really incredible work. I have to admit, your sinisterness is pretty amazing."

"Thank you, my boy. At least one youth still appreciates me."

"Is that why you're doing this? You think people don't appreciate you?" I asked.

"You wouldn't understand. You don't know what it's like to be famous and then lose it all."

"I'm the lead singer of a band. We won a Battle of the Bands contest. We played in front of thousands of people. When I went back to school in September, the same kids still picked on me. I still got knocked out by dodge balls moving at speeds that seemed inhuman. But you don't see me trying to ruin my nemesis so I feel better about myself."

Jimmy was about to respond, but all of our attention shifted to a pounding on the door.

"This has been a great conversation," Jimmy said, mindlessly, his eyes locked on the door in high alert.

"Maybe it's room service," the security guard said.

"I *would* like some more of those chocolates on my

pillow," Jimmy said to himself, then yelled, "Just put the chocolate under the door!"

The pounding continued. The door shook as if someone kicked it.

"Bert, be ready," Jimmy said.

Jimmy picked up Thor's hammer, as Bert walked toward the door, slowly.

Before Bert made it to the door, it burst open with a crack, quickly followed by C.T.'s body hurling through the air. C.T. let out a scream and then crash landed onto the tile floor. He slid across the wet floor, his head crashing into a wooden dresser.

CHAPTER 19

C.T. lay in a heap on the floor, not moving.

"Well, that was one heck of an entrance," Jimmy said.

"C.T.! Are you okay?" I yelled.

He didn't answer.

"Is he dead?" Bert asked, concerned.

"No, he just looks like he's unconscious," Jimmy said, annoyed, while studying C.T.

"Well, at least his wounds are on ice," Bert said.

"Now what?" Elvira asked, her eyes wide with concern.

"Oh, this is just fabulous," Jimmy said, his face breaking out into a huge smile. "My plan is working even better than I had planned. I was gonna knock his dumb face out back-stage and that little weasel, Kyle, too. He just knocked himself out."

"What do you want me to do?" Bert asked.

"Tie his hands up and leave him there. Did he bring any chocolate? Check his pockets," Jimmy ordered.

Bert leaned down and emptied C.T.'s pockets. "Nothing."

"Can you float me a dollar?" Jimmy asked.

"You owe me like twelve bucks," Bert said, annoyed.

"Nine."

"Eleven."

"Whatever. Just give me a dollar. My blood sugar's low. You can't expect me to take down the previously-great C.T. Walsh on an empty stomach, can you?"

"I guess not," Bert said, producing a dollar.

Jimmy looked at Elvira and asked, "Any update on the password? How long until we crack it?"

"There's no telling. It will definitely be cracked by morning."

"Morning? The press conference is right around the corner! We need the password now!"

"Why don't we just ask him for it?" Bert asked.

Jimmy raised an eyebrow. He bent down and slapped C.T. in the face.

"Not the money maker," C.T. groaned.

"Hey, what's your password for your laptop? We need it to save the world."

"Don't give it to them, C.T.!" I yelled. I was the only one of my crew without a duct-taped mouth.

"Shut him up," Jimmy said to Bert.

"Don't do it!" I yelled again.

Before I could say anything else, Bert's ginormous hands were in on my face, forcing the duct tape onto me. I tried to bite him, but, of course, I missed.

I heard Jimmy ask again, "What's your password?"

C.T. mumbled, "Farts1234."

Elvira typed it into the laptop. "Nope."

"Is it a capital F? What about an exclamation point?" Jimmy asked.

"Capital," C.T. groaned.

"Nope. Didn't work,"

Jimmy leaned over C.T.'s motionless body. "Tell us or the kids get it!"

C.T. didn't answer.

"What's the password?" Jimmy asked, viciously.

C.T. farted. I would say it was a Barking Tree Frog, but Jimmy jumped back after having been leaning over C.T.'s butt.

"Could that be it?" Jimmy asked, scratching his head. "Is it voice activated or maybe fart activated?" He looked at Elvira. "Make a note- when we get home, I want a fart-activated password system for all that I hold dear!"

"What if you don't have to fart? How will you unlock it?"

"That's the dumbest thing I've ever heard. I always have to fart." Jimmy's face soured. "Oh, God. That stinks." He reached over and grabbed a bowl of potpourri. He stood over C.T. and dumped the bowl's contents onto C.T.'s butt. Jimmy shook his head. "That's the best I can do. He's a disgusting creature." He looked at Elvira. "Now you know why I despise him so."

A ding echoed from C.T.'s laptop.

"What was that?" Jimmy asked.

"The password has been hacked!" Elvira said.

"Find the files and release them," Jimmy said, and followed with an evil cackle.

"What are you going to do?" Bert asked.

"Tell everyone they can get the new series for free and then ruin his squeaky-as-a-fart-clean reputation."

"I don't think that's how the saying goes, boss," Elvira said.

"What was the password, by the way?"

"Fartsarefun18."

"What an idiot."

"What should I do, boss?" Bert asked.

"You have to stay here. Watch these kids."

"What should I do with them?"

"I don't know. Put a movie on or something."

"Is PG-13 okay?"

"I don't care. I have to go. Don't forget to pack my cape from the closet!"

"What about the dress?" Bert asked.

"What dress?"

"The disguise. Do you want it?"

"I don't plan on wearing it again," Jimmy said, rolling his eyes.

Bert asked, "Are you sure? It matches your eyes and your skin tone beautifully."

Jimmy shook his head, stepped over C.T. and exited the room, fumbling with the half-broken door before disappearing with the parting words, "I'm gonna ruin you!" His cackle echoed through the halls.

I could read over Elvira's shoulder. She had found the files and was uploading them to a website. The screen read, 'Upload 30% complete.'

"Ugh. The hotel wi-fi is sooo slow. We should've paid for the high speed. Cheap Jimmy."

We had to stop this. We had been through too much to lose now. I had an idea.

"Shmorgleflufenhmeeemeee!"

"What?" Bert asked, walking toward me. He tore the duct tape from my face, yet again. It was a wonder I still had skin.

"Owww!"

"What is it, kid?"

"There's one little issue. We all just had lunch. With no parental supervision. I had a huge soda. I could barely carry it. It was bigger than a tub of popcorn at the movies."

"What's your point?"

"My point, Raul, is that I have to pee."

"Raul...I like that."

"Just let him pee in his pants," Elvira said over her shoulder.

"No way! That's inhumane! Even prisoners in jail get to pee in a toilet," I said.

"I got it covered," Bert said.

He cut the ties on my hands from the chair and pushed me forward toward the bedroom door.

I scanned the room, trying to figure out what I would do to escape. I had to take Bert out and either free one of my friends or take out the lady hacker, too. But how? He was about three times bigger than the biggest football player in my school, Nick DeRozan.

Bert led me through the bedroom to the bathroom. He pushed me into the room and stood in the doorway, leaning on the frame.

I frowned at him. "Can I have a little privacy? I'm a minor. Don't you think it's a little weird that you are gonna watch me pee?"

"Kinda."

"What if I have to go poopoo?"

"Ok," Bert said. He stepped out of the bathroom and pulled the door mostly shut.

As I peed, I looked around the room. I saw towels, tissues, and a hair dryer. There was also a bottle of Jimmy's cologne. I looked at the bottle. It read 'Eau de toilette'. It figures he would have a cologne that referenced the toilet. What else was there? A shower curtain. A shower curtain! Well, shower curtain rod! I remembered my battle with Daddy Darth.

I flushed the toilet and then grabbed the cologne. I popped the top and held it in my hand.

I called out to Bert, "Just gonna wash my hands. I don't want to get any pee on you."

I flipped on the water, hoping to mute the sound of what I was going to do next. I reached for the shower curtain rod and tugged on it. The rod squeaked as the rubber skidded across the tile. The left side of the rod tipped toward the tub, the shower curtain rings rushing for the end with the scraping of metal on metal. I decided to let the curtain slip all the way off. It was a nice, solid rod. My heart raced, hoping that Bert hadn't heard it. Unfortunately, he did.

I turned as the door opened and Burt peeked his head in.

"What the heck are you doing?"

"I tripped and pulled this down. Nerd problems."

"Oh, here let me help you." Bert stepped forward.

I weighed the curtain rod in my hand. I hoped it was strong enough to knock Bert out. I was about to find out. As he took a step toward me, I held the cologne bottle up to his face and said, "In your face, sucka!" And then sprayed the cologne. Nothing happened. Not even a little spritz. He grabbed my wrist, but I kept spraying. After three sprays, it seemed to be fully primed and a glorious spritz of Eau de Toilette burst forth from the bottle and connected for a direct hit of Bert's eyes.

Bert's high-pitched scream was less than helpful, as it echoed off the bathroom tiles. That was less of a problem, though, when compared to the thud his body made when it hit the floor after the brain-chattering clank of the curtain rod connecting with his skull. Mr. Muscalini, my gym teacher, would be proud. Not necessarily of the assault (but hey, it was self-defense, since I was kidnapped at the time) but of my baseball power swing. The problem was the entire room shook and I was pretty certain that the hacker was coming.

I heard her say, "What the- Bert? What happened?"

"Umm, I think Bert's having a heart attack! Call 9-1-1!"

I held the curtain rod in my hand as Elvira entered, her face registering panic. She held a phone in her hand. She looked at me and then at Burt. I stood at the ready to attack, but I didn't want to if I didn't have to.

"Why are you holding a curtain rod and why does his

face have a huge red mark across it in the shape of a curtain rod?"

I looked down at the rod in my hand and then at Bert's face and said, "Umm, because of this!"

I swung the curtain rod. She ducked and grabbed it with her hand. My eyes widened in shock, as we struggled for control of the weapon. I stomped on her foot with my heel as hard as I could. It usually proved to be a decent delay tactic when fighting with Derek. She doubled over, but didn't let go of the rod. I slammed my heel down on her other foot. She shrieked in pain, as she let go of the rod. I grabbed it with two hands and swung it as hard as I could, right at the backs of her legs. The force of the blow swept her from her feet. She landed on her back with a thud. It didn't shake the entire hotel like Bert did, but still, it shook. I ran from the room, closing the door behind me. I'm not sure why, since I couldn't lock her out, but I guess it gave me extra time.

I quickly untied Ben and Luke and they helped me untie the rest of the crew. It was perfect timing because the door flew open and revealed a hobbling, very angry hacker. She held an iron in one hand and a lamp in another.

"I think we're good with the natural lighting in here," I said.

Ben grabbed the hotel phone and picked it up. He dialed 9-1-1, as the hacker surged toward him.

Ben slammed the phone down and yelled, "No!"

I grabbed the lamp and struggled with Elvira. The others joined in, as we all grappled for control of the decorating weapons.

Ben hung up the phone and tried again. "There's no dial tone!"

"I cut the line. Only cell phones work in here and yours

are locked in the safe." The hacker smiled, kicked three of my crew off her iron-holding hand, and then surged forward, attempting to press my wrinkly face with the iron.

I ducked. "Is that the cotton setting? I'm more silky, myself."

"We have numbers!" Sophie yelled.

"Great! I can burp the alphabet!" Luke yelled.

As the hacker swung wildly at us, none of us were able to get close.

"No! We outnumber her. Surround her and attack!" Sophie yelled.

I was half impressed and half afraid that my girlfriend was such a fierce warlord. She grabbed a floor lamp with both hands like a bo staff, ripping the cord out of the wall in the process. I wondered if she was inspired by the day at Comic Con with all the super heroes. The hacker swung her own smaller lamp at everyone, and jabbed the iron at anyone who stepped into her circle.

Our group surrounded the hacker in a giant circle. Sophie had her floor lamp. Ben held the phone and cord. Luke had a book about local artwork. Cheryl was hunkered down by the mini fridge chucking water bottles and candy packets at Elvira. Just Charles had a pillow. In his defense, it was a pretty big one.

The hacker was ferocious. Perhaps sensing impending doom and a lengthy prison sentence, she fought like a lioness protecting her young. Pictures were broken. Fake plants were uprooted. And every M&M previously in the fridge was crushed on the floor, creating a seemingly tasty technicolor floor covering. Unfortunately, I didn't get a chance to taste it. I'd rather that than the never-cleaned carpet beneath it.

Our group wasn't filled with athletes and certainly not

warriors. I didn't know how long we would last. And then it came to me.

"Nerd Knockdown!" I yelled.

"What the heck is that?" Sophie asked.

"Just keep fighting," I said, still struggling with the hacker over a lamp. She had serious strength. Or I didn't have any.

I knew Ben, Just Charles, and Luke would know what the Nerd Knockdown was. Ben was first to act. He dove onto the floor behind the hacker and started wrapping the phone cord around her legs. The hacker felt the tight cord wrap around her, and kicked her feet out, stretching the cord to its limits, but it didn't break. Switching gears, she swung the lamp behind her, connecting with Ben's shoulder. He grunted and writhed in pain. I took one Goliath step, planning to jump off the remains of the coffee table and onto the hacker, but I missed, tripped, and stumbled on top of Ben. It was still helpful as Luke, Sophie, and Just Charles attacked, while Cheryl had resorted to throwing ice cubes from the freezer at the hacker. She wasn't big on the one-to-one combat, apparently.

The triple onslaught was enough to overwhelm Elvira. She stumbled back, helped by a savage pillow blow to her face by Just Charles. Elvira screamed as she tried to step back, but the combo of the phone cord and the pile of nerds that Ben and I had assembled behind her feet and knees did the trick. She tripped over us and stumbled back with a groan. She hit her head on a dresser as she fell back and lay quiet, but still breathing on the floor.

'That was easy," I said, getting up from the floor.

"You didn't get hit with a lamp," Ben said.

"Umm, it's about to get less easy." I looked up at the hulking Bert standing in the door way. His eyes were red, seemingly from the cologne, and he had a long red mark running down his face.

I only had one move. Thor's hammer. I summoned it by reaching out my hand and yelling (you guessed it), "Hammer!"

The hammer soared from the counter top through the air into my palm. There is some debate as to whether or not the hammer flew on its own or if Cheryl threw it to me, but as far as I was concerned, I was Thor, God of Thunder. With terrible hand-eye coordination. The hammer soared past my closed fist and smashed into the window with a crack. The window spiderwebbed as the hammer bounced onto the floor. Oops.

"Austin, look out!" Sophie yelled.

Bert surged his oversized body toward me. I dove for the hammer, nearly smashing through the window to the less-than-enticing concrete below. I grabbed the hammer and threw it as hard as I could at Bert's rapidly approaching oversized head. It connected with a crack. His eyes rolled inward and then back in his head as his body went limp on top of me.

I gasped for air as I struggled to roll Bert off me, but he was just too heavy, even for the mighty, nerdy Thor. But my team was right behind me. They pulled. They grunted. I think Luke gave him a supersonic wedgie, which Bert most certainly deserved. And finally, they rolled the horrific henchman off me. I inhaled glorious air for what seemed like the first time in forever. The only thing that wasn't horrible about the whole experience was that Bert's eyes smelled terrific. His Eau de Toilette was quality stuff. Note to self: add it to my Christmas list.

"Let's tie these clowns up," I said, between breaths.

"With what?" Just Charles said, looking around the room. "Everything's broken."

"Use all the cords from the irons, lights, phones. Whatever you can find."

"We need our phones," Sophie said.

"I know. I'm dying over here," Luke said. "I need to play Toon Blast."

"We should also call the cops," Sophie said, rolling her eyes.

"Oh, yeah. That, too," Luke said with a smile.

Sophie, Luke, and I ran into the bedroom. Sophie pulled open the closet door, revealing a small safe with a number pad.

"Farts 1234?" I asked.

"How about just the 1234?" Sophie asked. She typed it in. After it clicked, she yelled, "Yes!"

Luke opened the safe door and pulled out the laundry bag of phones.

"We need to get medical attention for C.T. as soon as possible," I said.

CHAPTER 20

While I tried to make sense of everything that had just happened, Ben called out from the other room. "C.T. is waking up!"

We reassembled our phones. Cheryl called 9-1-1 while the rest of us circled C.T. as he sat up on the floor. He looked around the destroyed hotel room, rubbing his head.

"What the heck did you guys do in here? Must've been some kind of party."

Luke and I held out our hands to help C.T. to his feet. He stood up with a grunt and then walked over to the still unconscious Bert.

"That's a big dude. Did I knock him out when I crashed through the door?"

I looked up at C.T. and said, "Unfortunately, the only person you knocked out when you crashed through the door was yourself."

"That's harsh, dude. You guys took him out?" C.T. said. He leaned over Bert, checking him out. "Impressive, kids. And he smells spectacular." C.T. stood up and asked, "Have you smelled him?"

Before we could answer, there was a knock at the door. Then we heard Kyle say, "What the-"

C.T. walked over to the door and opened it. "Welcome to the party, Kyle!"

Kyle stepped in and looked around, horrified.

"Why aren't you at the press conference?" C.T. asked.

Kyle didn't answer for a moment. He appeared to be stunned by all of the destruction. It was impressive. There were broken tables, chairs, and lamps, a cracked window, crushed candy everywhere, puddles with half-melted ice, and pillow feathers strewn about. Oh, and two people tied up with phone chords and lamp wires. It was a lot to take in.

"You're late. You never showed up," Kyle said, still looking around in awe.

"We have to get back there and stop Jimmy," I said.

"Jimmy O'Beans? He's involved in this? What's he going to do?"

"Well, he was going to release the series to the world for free, but we stopped that, but he says he's going to ruin C.T.'s reputation," Sophie said.

"I tell fart jokes. What could he possibly do to ruin my reputation?" C.T. said, laughing.

Kyle looked C.T. up and down. C.T.'s hair was messy, his shirt untucked, and his face had a huge red mark across his cheek. "Are you okay?"

C.T. nodded. "You know what hurts the worst? My finger. He shook out his hand. "I jammed my finger when I fell. Can you pull it to stretch it out?"

Kyle pulled C.T.'s finger. A fart ripped from C.T.'s jeans.

"Gotcha! Again. That never gets old."

"It smells like something's old," Sammie said.

"Go take a whiff of Bert over there," C.T. said. "And add his cologne to my Christmas list," he said to Kyle. C.T.

looked at me and said, "Austin, I'd like you to take Jimmy's cologne as a token of my appreciation."

"That's mighty generous of you, C.T."

"That's not all I'm going to do for you, guys. Thank you for getting my laptop back before they ruined my career by uploading all of my work of the past two years."

"Laptop! Uploading! Problem!" I yelled. "We need to stop the upload, if it isn't out into cyberspace already!"

I rushed to the laptop and opened it. "Ahh, farts! It's at 96%. How do I shut this down? There's no cancel button," I said in a panic.

C.T. and Just Charles rushed over to me.

Just Charles said, "You sure you can't shut it down?" He scanned the screen and then pressed escape. Nothing happened.

"Yeah, I hadn't thought of that."

C.T. looked out at the window. "Hey, that's a nice pool out there. Kyle messed up on this one. Our pool isn't that nice."

"97%! We'll worry about his hotel selection capabilities later!" I yelled.

C.T. picked up Thor's Hammer, smiled at it, and then smashed it through the window. Glass crumbled and clunked to the floor and outside to the pavement.

"What the- 98%!" I yelled.

C.T. grabbed the laptop in front of me, shut it, and then hurled it out the window like a frisbee. My mouth dropped open. The laptop sailed over the concrete walkway as it plummeted to the ground, and then splashed down into the pool below.

A bunch of sun bathers looked up at us, wondering what the heck was going on. C.T. waved and gave them a thumbs up.

"I think I broke a world record. Do you know anybody who has thrown a laptop that far? Certainly, nobody's done it after breaking a window with Thor's hammer," C.T. said, smiling. He turned to the group. "Nice work, everyone. We probably could've just cut the wi-fi on the laptop, so it didn't complete the upload. But still, you probably should've thought of that one, Aus."

"Sorry," I said, with my best sheesh face.

"I didn't really like that laptop, anyway. Not a big deal. I mean, I did have the coordinates to the Lost City of Atlantis on there, but what are you gonna do? Anywho, we should probably skedaddle."

"What does that even mean?" Ben asked.

"We gotta move! We need to take down Jimmy," I said.

C.T. thrust his fist in the air. "Team Fartstorm Unite!"

"Yeah, I don't want to be on Team Fartstorm," Sophie said.

"Okay, it's a work in progress," C.T. said, shrugging.

Luke asked excitedly, "How about Lit Fart?"

"Oooh, I like that," C.T. said, nodding.

"It was almost our band name," Luke said.

"No, it was never even close," I said.

"That's your loss, Aus," C.T. said, shaking his head.

I shook my head back. "Let's agree to disagree, C.T."

"Well, let's move," C.T. said, rushing to the door.

We followed him into the hallway, leaving the criminals behind.

"Ahhh, freedom!" I yelled.

"What are we gonna do about them?" Sophie asked, pointing back to the room.

A man turned the corner, dressed as The Flash. He stopped dead in his tracks when he saw us. "What the-"

"Barry Allen!" C.T. yelled. "What an honor. Can you do us a favor?"

"Umm, sure," The faux Flash said, seemingly not so sure, as he stared into the destroyed hotel room.

"Inside that room are two criminals. Can you watch over them until the police arrive?"

"Will do, sirs! And ladies!" The Flash rushed into the room and then turned around. "What do I tell the cops?"

"Tell them that the big dude broke everything!" Just Charles said. "Oh, and they were responsible for the theft of C.T. Walsh's laptop!"

"Thanks, Barry," C.T. said, with a thumbs up.

"You got it!" The Flash yelled.

CHAPTER 21

We headed out quickly, running as fast as we could back to the convention center. It was too risky to take a pedicab after the last mishap. The crowds were still huge. I noticed security guards at most of the doors. We took a slight detour and chose an unguarded one.

It was mayhem inside. Only a few steps in, someone yelled, "C.T.! Can I have an autograph?"

Within thirty seconds, C.T. was being swarmed by autograph and picture seekers.

He took a deep breath and started signing.

"We gotta go, C.T.," I said, hoping to give everyone the hint.

"Sorry, guys," he said, but kept taking pens from people to sign autograph pads.

He looked at me and said, "Go. I'll meet you there."

"Just one more," a kid pleaded, thrusting her autograph book into C.T.'s hands.

"Okay, but I really have to go. It's official police business."

"You're a cop?" someone asked.

"Well, no, so it's technically unofficial police business, but trust me, it's police business."

We left C.T. behind and continued on to the press conference. We dodged, weaved, and pushed our way through the large crowds. Ben was by my side with the rest of the crew in front.

Ben pushed me hard on my shoulder.

"What's going on, dude?" I asked, annoyed, but then looked over to see a security guard staring at me, not too far from Ben.

"We gotta move. You've just been made," Ben said.

I looked back to see the security guard talking into his shoulder walkie-talkie, following us. It was worse than I thought. I wondered if my picture was on a Wanted poster somewhere. I hoped they didn't use one of Sophie's pictures of my nose hair.

We pushed through the crowd. And then I had an idea.

"Let's crawl," I said.

"Okay," Ben said, reluctantly.

We dropped to our knees and started crawling through the crowd.

We got a few strange stares from the people above us, but no real issues.

"Let's circle back behind him. He won't expect that."

"Nice," Ben said.

We crawled off to the side and waited for a few minutes until the security guard passed.

"We need costumes," I said. "Or at least I do."

Eventually, we found a clear area where the rest of our crew was waiting for us.

"What happened?" Sophie asked.

"They're looking for me. We had to lose a security guard. I think I need a costume."

"A disguise," Sammie corrected.

"True," I said.

"How are we gonna get them?" Ben asked.

"Nobody has enough cash for that," Just Charles said. "In hindsight, I might've bought too many snacks."

"Let's beat somebody up and take them," Luke said.

"Who are we gonna beat up?" Sammie asked, shaking her head.

"Like how about that guy with the fake muscle costume?" Luke said. "That'll be a good disguise."

Sophie said, "That's a full-grown man and his hulking muscles are real."

And the guy next to him, while not as muscular, was tall, and dressed as Captain America. Hulk was covered in green makeup from head to toe and wore nothing but a pair of ripped jean shorts. Or maybe it wasn't makeup. It could've been the real Hulk for all I knew. And Captain America wore a mask, so we had no idea who he was, but the two of them looked at us like they knew who we were.

My pulse quickened. With everything going on, I didn't know if they were a risk or not, but then I heard the Hulk say, "Dodgeball good, Davenport! Hulk loves dodgeball!"

I took a closer look. How did this guy know my name? There was only one person I knew with that many muscles who knew my distaste for dodgeball. "Mr. Muscalini?" I asked.

"I am The Hulk," the man said, gruffly.

Captain America took off his mask, revealing the chiseled face of one Eugene Zorch, our beloved custodian.

The Hulk's shoulders slumped. "Oh, come on, Steve. You said we would stay in costume the whole time," Mr. Muscalini whined.

"You spent half the time in the bathroom," Zorch said, annoyed.

"I had a stomach ache!"

I didn't need to know that Mr. Muscalini was *the* Hulk that clogged the toilet.

"Well, it ruined everything," Zorch said, crossing his arms.

"Who's Steve?" Sophie asked.

"Steve Rogers, Captain America," Mr. Muscalini said.

"Oh, you guys are really serious," Sammie said.

Mr. Muscalini looked over at Zorch and said, "Well, one of us is."

Zorch ignored Mr. Muscalini. "How's it going, guys? Enjoying the show?"

"You could say that," I said. "But it wouldn't be true."

"What's the matter?" Mr. Muscalini asked, concerned.

"Well, we're trying to solve a mystery," Ben said.

"Gordo!" Mr. Muscalini said. "I see you haven't done any of the summer workouts I painstakingly designed for you."

Ben shifted from foot to foot. "Umm, well. I've done some of them."

"Something must be off with your protein consumption."

"We don't have time for this," I said.

"There's always time for protein," Mr. Muscalini responded, angrily.

"C.T. Walsh's laptop was stolen."

"The author? That's one handsome man," Mr. Muscalini said.

Zorch shrugged, "Meh."

"What can we do to help?" Mr. Muscalini asked.

I thought about it for a moment. "We need some cold

hard cash. Well, we also take credit cards. Do you take PayPal or Venmo?" I asked Sophie.

"Not currently, no."

I looked back at my two teachers dressed up in cosplay and said, "Okay, so just cash or credit. We need disguises."

"To do what with?" Zorch asked.

"It's better that you not know. I'll pay you back."

"You've said that to me too many times, Austin," Zorch said, shaking his head with a smile.

Sophie shook my arm. I looked over at her.

"We gotta go," she said, looking across the room.

"What's wrong?" I asked. And then I saw Sergeant Villone heading our way.

"She's right," I said. "We gotta go. Pronto."

"Are you on the run, Austin?" Zorch asked, concerned.

"No, just a strange coincidence. And tell him we went the other way!" I yelled.

I slipped into the crowd moving toward the press conference room. We made it there without getting arrested, which is usually how I like to arrive at places. I grabbed Sophie's hand and pulled her through the swarms of people in the packed room. It was an auditorium, much like the panel discussion we were in earlier. There were at least twenty rows of seats and people lining the walls, sitting in chairs or standing.

Jimmy, the counterfeit C.T., stood up on the stage in front of the podium with his hat and C.T. mask on.

"Welcome, everyone," Jimmy said, gruffly. "My apologies. I think I'm losing my voice. "It's an exciting day to celebrate me. How about some applause for C.T.? Come on! Show some appreciation!"

A bunch of people clapped, while others chattered away, not sure why C.T. was being so arrogant. I knew it was because Jimmy was trying to make C.T. out to be a bad guy. He might blame his farts on other people or amphibians that bark like a dog, but he's not a bad guy.

Sophie and I jostled to the front of the room with my crew not too far behind. We stood to the left side of the crowd, right next to the first column of seats. There were free-standing chairs lining the wall next to us as well.

"We have to do something," Sophie whispered.

I nodded. I looked around, trying to come up with a plan. My genius brain was empty.

Jimmy said, "I've made so much money selling you fools my terrible fart jokes, frankly, I'm bored with it all. I'm giving my new series away for free. You can download it online!"

Some of the crowd cheered. The rest looked around, seemingly surprised and confused. I kind of felt bad for them. They didn't know we already stopped that from happening, but still.

And then I had an idea. A photographer right next to us stood up to take a picture of the counterfeit C.T. I grabbed his chair and pulled it toward me.

"What are you doing?" Sophie whisper-yelled.

"You just said we have to do something!" I whisper-yelled back.

In the meantime, the photographer attempted to sit down, his chair no longer lined up with his butt cheeks. He fell to the floor with a grunt. His camera fell out of his hands and cracked onto the floor.

"Oops," I said. I quickly stood up on the chair and addressed the crowd. "He's a fraud!" I yelled, pointing at Jimmy.

Jimmy looked at me, his eyes bulging. The crowd went quiet. Suddenly, I was very self-conscious. I didn't know what else to say. Everyone stared at me, including the two cops that stood on the side of each stairway up to the stage.

One of cops looked down at the paper in his hand, grabbed his earpiece and whispered something. I tried to read his lips, but couldn't. When he looked back up at me, I knew it wasn't good. It also could've been from when he yelled, "You there! You're under arrest for the theft of C.T. Walsh's laptop."

Ahhh, farts!

CHAPTER 22

My heart pounded. The crowd chatter rose, nobody sure about what was going to happen. The cops made their way toward me, as I tried to figure out a plan to make my getaway. The fake C.T. looked down from the stage, as the crowd had stopped paying attention to him. All eyes were on me.

Fake C.T. yelled, "That's him! That's the perpetrator. Seize him!"

Some dude dressed as Batman tried to grab me. Sophie grabbed my hand and pulled me from the chair.

"Guys! I'm innocent! I swear! That's not the real C.T.! He's an imposter!" I slipped from Batman's grip, the force and momentum turning me around. I found myself in the chest of a less-than Incredible Hulk. Unfortunately, it wasn't Mr. Muscalini.

"Thieves make Hulk angry!" The Hulk grabbed my shoulders with each hand and lifted me off the ground. He held me for the cops, despite my kicking and screaming.

"No!" I yelled. It wasn't overly helpful.

"That's Jimmy O'Beans!" Sophie yelled. "He's an imposter!"

The cop slapped the handcuff on my left wrist, but we were all distracted by the Tarzan-like roar coming from the side of the stage.

The Hulk dropped me, as the entire crowd stared up onto the stage. C.T. emerged from behind the side curtain, swinging on a rope.

His eyes widened and his roar morphed into a toddler shriek. I'm not sure where his landing target was, but I'm pretty certain he didn't hit it, because he smashed into the podium instead. Jimmy O'Beans jumped back, surprised. C.T. lay on the wood floor, intermingled with planks of podium.

"Oh, God. Not again," I said.

"Is he conscious?" Sophie asked, concerned.

C.T. popped up. "I'm okay. I'm okay. I think I heard a Barking Tree Frog, though. They're all over the place. There's two of them!" He pointed off stage.

In the mayhem, I was able to wriggle free from the police officer's grip and rush past a group of people crowding the aisles, all standing up to see what was happening up on stage. I pulled Sophie behind me. The crowd all strained to see what was going on. It was difficult to navigate the packed room, but it was easier for us than the cops who wanted to arrest me.

I looked up on stage to see C.T. and Jimmy, staring each other down, standing face to face.

"There's two of them," the bogus Batman said.

My grandpappy always used to say, "If you can beat 'em, become 'em," Jimmy said.

"That's not a saying," C.T. said.

Jimmy pushed C.T. in the chest with both hands. "If my grandpappy said it, it's a saying!"

"I didn't know it was possible for two people to be this handsome," C.T. said, taking a step back. "But not for long, sucka!" C.T. reached back with his left hand in a fist and let it fly.

He connected with Jimmy's face, knocking him to the floor and his hat beside him. I could see the latex peeling at Jimmy's hair line. Jimmy grabbed his face with one hand and used his other to get back to his feet.

"Why are you doing this?" C.T. asked.

"I'm the prince and you're the pauper."

"Did he say pooper?" I asked Sophie.

"We're all poopers," C.T. said, as they circled other.

"Pauper, you idiot!" Jimmy yelled.

"Oh, like the prince and the pauper. I get it. You're very

witty. I don't really know why your career is tanking." C.T. shrugged.

"My career is not tanking! It's just a bit of a rough patch."

"Now what, Jimmy?" C.T. asked.

"Now, we fight to the death!" Jimmy yelled.

C.T. raised an eyebrow. "Yeah, I'm not doin' that."

"Then we fight to unconsciousness!"

"Yeah, that just doesn't have the same ring to it."

Jimmy put his hands on his hips. "Are you sure about the whole death thing?"

"Pretty certain. Now what?"

"Not sure," Jimmy said, with a sneer.

"Stop sneering at me."

"I'm not sneering at you."

"You totally are."

"Fine, I sneered at you. And I'll sneer at you whenever I want."

C.T. chuckled. "Sneer. Such a funny word. Sneer, sneer, sneer, sneer, sneer."

Some dude yelled, "Does anybody know what's going on?"

"That's Jimmy O'Beans!" Sophie yelled.

"Which one?" the jerky Batman who tried to capture me, yelled.

His costumed counterpart, Robin, asked, "Both of them?"

Batman shook his head, disapprovingly.

I didn't know it at the time, but Just Charles grabbed a giant soda from a fellow guest, tore off the top, and downed it. Then he tore a bag of skittles from someone else and chowed down on them. He caught up to us in the crowd and grabbed my arm with a crazed look in his eye.

"Oh, no!"

"What?" Sophie asked.

Cheryl called from back in the crowd, "Charles, no! Come back to me!"

Sophie and I, along with the few people around us, watched in shock as Evil Chuck whirled around in a circle, perhaps even faster than Superman did when he changed his clothes in a phone booth. He stopped and looked at us, his eyes almost glowing.

"Charles, What's wrong with you?" Sophie asked, but I knew.

"I'm not Charles. I'm Evil Chuck!" He pushed his way through the crowd with an evil cackle, heading for the stage.

A dude with a backwards hat and some beard scruff said, "Oh my God! That was amazing! Did we really just witness the origin story of a real villain?"

"It's not his origin story. He's terrorized before, but I guess this is his first time in public," I said in awe.

"I want to create a comic book about him!" the dude said, handing me his business card. "Give me a call!"

"Yeah," I said, mindlessly. I pulled Sophie toward the stage.

"I have to get up there." But without Evil Chuck's villain power, I didn't have the ability. And then I figured out my plan of attack. "Mr. Muscalini!" I yelled to him in the crowd just ahead of me. He had arrived there with Zorch, still dressed as Captain America.

He looked at me like I just crushed his soul. "I'm the Hulk! The Incredible Hulk!"

"Incredible Hulk! I need you to get me up there," I said, pointing to the stage that had a dozen people wrestling on it, including C.T., Jimmy, and Evil Chuck. The last time I saw a melee that large was when I instigated a food fight between the baseball and track teams on meatballs marinara day. It was awesome.

We made our way over to Mr. Muscalini. He looked at me seriously and said, "There's only one way to get you up there. And it's gonna hurt."

"I know," I said.

"Anything you want to say about that handcuff on your wrist?" Zorch asked, concerned.

"Misunderstanding?" I said, shrugging. I looked at Mr. Muscalini. "The time is now."

Zorch said, "It's too dangerous."

"There's no way around it, Captain." I saluted him.

Sophie leaned over and kissed me on the cheek. "Good luck."

I almost fell over and that was before The Hulk implemented our plan.

"You ready?" Mr. Muscalini asked.

"Yep."

Zorch handed me his shield. "Take this. You may need it."

"Thanks."

Mr. Muscalini stepped behind me, grabbed me by my t-shirt behind my neck and my jeans at my lower back. Mr. Muscalini lifted me off the floor, rocked me back and forth twice, and then on the third time, tossed me through the air with a room-shaking scream, "Hulk smash!"

The first half of the trip was pretty awesome. I soared through the air over a variety of people pretending to be superhero characters: Batman, Robin, Black Widow, Spider-man, Green Arrow, and even the flying Superman himself. They looked up at me in awe.

"He's flying!" Robin yelled.

Everyone stopped their fighting and watched in wonder,

as I defied gravity en route to the stage. The second half of the flight was not as exciting. Gravity kicked in and I realized I didn't have a landing plan. I clutched Captain America's shield with both hands and curled myself up into a ball inside its circle. I landed on the stage with a huge thwack, slid for a few feet, and then rolled off into a crowd in the midst of a kerfuffle.

I looked back to my crew and gave a half-hearted thumbs up. I was glad I still had it attached. My entire body throbbed. As soon as the wonder of my flight wore off, the entire room was back at it. Perhaps even more aggressive than before.

There was a less-than-dynamic Batman and Robin duo on the stage, wrestling. Batman yelled, "You're the worst sidekick! Superman never has to put up with nonsense like yours!"

The phony Hulk that had handed me off to the cops was grappling with someone dressed as The Thing from The Fantastic Four. A Wonder Woman older than Luke's lunch date was fending off items thrown at her with her plastic wrist armor. And there were too many head locks, noogies, and charlie horses to count. And that was just from the adults.

C.T.'s assistant, Kyle, found me in the pile and dragged me out.

"Thanks," I said, but I looked over to see Jimmy and C.T. still going at it. "Look!" I yelled.

Jimmy slugged C.T. in the gut. He doubled over, but when Jimmy surged forward to finish his attack, C.T. unleashed a massive uppercut that caught Jimmy in the chin. He stumbled back, his teeth seemingly still chattering.

Jimmy looked at C.T. and his face dropped. He grabbed his left arm. "Oooh, my arm. It's tingling. I think I'm having a heart attack. I've never...seen...Paris."

C.T. moved closer, concerned. "Jimmy, you okay?"

"Yaaaahhh!" Jimmy screamed and then blasted C.T. with a wicked ridge hand to his nose.

C.T.'s hands instinctively grabbed his face. "Not the money maker!" he yelled, as he fell in slow motion.

"You fell for the oldest trick in the book!" Jimmy yelled. He jumped in the air over C.T.'s body and yelled, "Flying elbow!" Jimmy crashed on top of C.T., his elbow landing with a smack on C.T.'s shoulder.

C.T. groaned and then yelled back, "Purple nurple, punk!" while surging forward with both hands ready for a deadly pinch and twist.

It was clear that neither of those two had any formal

fight training, but were brought up by watching wrestling or perhaps were tormented by older brothers.

Jimmy knocked C.T.'s hands away. They both rolled and returned to their feet.

"Come at me, bro!" C.T. yelled.

"I'm coming!"

"I know. I just told you to."

It was the weirdest fight I've ever seen in my life. And then it got stranger. My worst fear hit. The hacker and the henchman showed up on stage eying C.T.

Before I could do anything, my crew was up on stage with Mr. Muscalini and Zorch, both swatting nerdy comic bookers off the stage. A group of people rushed Jimmy's less-than-dynamic duo and attacked.

It was Wrestle Mania, only with people who had no idea how to wrestle.

"You lose, Jimmy!" C.T. yelled.

"Do I? Even if you win this battle, I've won the war. Your precious yet pathetic work has already been released to the world for free!"

"That's too bad. Too bad it never happened."

C.T. rushed Jimmy and tackled him. Jimmy turned to his stomach, while C.T. landed on Jimmy's back. He sat up and slipped his hands underneath Jimmy's chin.

"What never happened?" Jimmy said, through gritted teeth, while struggling against the most devastating wrestling move ever created, the Camel Clutch.

"The upload never happened!" C.T. said, laughing. "My laptop wanted to hit the pool."

"No!" Jimmy shrieked.

It looked like C.T. was going to finish the battle, but the hacker broke free from Luke and Ben holding onto his/her legs and feet, and knocked C.T. off Jimmy's back with a devastating kick to the shoulder.

I saw Bert running toward Jimmy and C.T. with Thor's hammer in his hand. I had to do something. Luke was on his hands and knees, apparently still recovering from letting go of the hacker's leg. I ran toward Bert and jumped onto Luke's back, like back at the hotel with the coffee table. Only this time, it was worse. My foot collided with Luke's ribs. I stumbled over him and crashed into Bert's legs, and held on for dear life. Bert toppled over, stumbling toward the edge of the stage. He tried to stop himself by grabbing C.T. and Jimmy, but to no avail. We all fell off the front of the stage and crashed onto the people below, ultimately ending up on the floor.

C.T. and Jimmy clashed again. Bert joined in, slapping C.T. into a choke hold from behind. C.T.'s face went red. I sank my teeth into Jimmy's thigh with a vicious attack. He screamed and smacked me in the head.

Things got kind of fuzzy for a minute, but I heard C.T. say between gasps, "You...smell...terrific!"

Bert didn't answer. He just squeezed harder.

C.T. was losing his marbles. He said, "Oooh, those stars are pretty."

Jimmy yelled, "Bert, are you wearing my cologne? That's my Eau de Toilette!"

While Bert was still trying to eliminate C.T.'s ability to breath, Jimmy attacked Bert in a rage.

"I told you- only I'm allowed to smell that good!" Jimmy punched Bert, who loosened his grip on C.T. and grappled with Jimmy, instead.

C.T. and I both came back to the present. We looked at Jimmy and Bert wrestling, not sure what to do.

"This is mayhem," C.T. said.

"Kinda reminds me of middle school."

C.T. looked around. "Tell me about it. How do we stop this? This is ridiculous."

Before I could answer, C.T. doubled over from a punch below the belt. He crumpled to his knees and then fell flat on his face with a high-pitched shriek. I looked down to see Bert and Jimmy riddling C.T. with punches.

I kicked Jimmy as hard as I could. He absorbed the brunt of my kick, but was able to grab my foot and toss it backward. I fell back onto my butt and then hit my head on a chair with a thud. I grabbed the back of my head in pain.

"Must. Help. C.T." I said, rolling to my knees. And then I saw it. I saw the weapon that would end this war. The weapon that had already gotten me out of a huge jam that day. Thor's hammer was underneath the seat next to me. I grabbed it and stood up.

C.T. and Jimmy were still wrestling on the floor, but Bert was now on his feet. He looked at me and smiled. At least I think he was smiling. Most of his teeth were missing.

I pointed to the front of the auditorium and yelled, "Look! A Barking Tree Frog!"

Bert turned his head to look, as I unleashed a vicious two-handed hammer attack to his noggin. It connected with a crack. Bert fell to his knees and then onto his face, adding insult to injury. I hoped three times was a charm.

My Darth Dad gave me a thumbs up while wrestling a Wookie, and yelled, "Nice job, son!"

C.T. took a right hook from Jimmy, spinning him around. I thought he might collapse, but he stumbled back. He smiled, missing two teeth, and said, "Having fun?"

I shook my head and tossed the hammer in the air. C.T. grabbed it and turned, ready to attack, but Jimmy was already delivering another knuckle sandwich.

"No!" I yelled. I surged toward C.T. and pushed him aside. He collided with the stage and collapsed to the ground, no doubt unconscious yet again.

Jimmy's eyes glowed with anger. With little warning, he unleashed a barrage of punches and kicks. I ducked and dodged. Thankfully, he was slowed by the battle he had just finished with C.T., so I was able to fend off his attack.

But my Darth Dad was less than thrilled. He pushed the Wookie aside and yelled, "My son!"

Before he could save me, Evil Chuck flew from the stage, his foot heading straight toward Jimmy's face. He connected with precision, knocking Jimmy out cold.

Evil Chuck landed superhero style, one knee and one fist on the ground.

The Vader Faker took two steps back, his eyes locked on Evil Chuck. For a moment, I thought Evil Chuck might attack, but then he shook his head violently, looked down at his hands, and turned to me.

I looked into Evil Chuck's eyes to see Just Charles staring back at me.

Confusion spread across his face. "What...happened? Why do my hands hurt?"

"You just saved the day."

"I did or Evil Chuck did?"

"You can't be evil if you saved the day."

Just Charles shrugged and then smiled.

Sophie rushed over to me and jumped into my arms. "I was so worried about you," she said.

I squeezed her tight, and then realized that C.T. was still unconscious. I put Sophie back down on the ground and turned to C.T. He lay next to Jimmy, starting to stir.

"Oh, no!" Sophie said.

We knelt down next to C.T. I asked, "Are you all right?" I shook his shoulder.

"Yeah, just get Jimmy's butt out of my face. He totally farted."

And that's when I knew he was gonna be okay.

CHAPTER 23

The thing about nerd fights is that they don't last particularly long. We don't have much stamina. Having already broken all the important nerd-fighting records, most of the melee participants were flat-out pooped by that point. People either just sat back down in their chairs or lay down right on the stage.

Back-up arrived for the cops and were sorting everything out. All participants were conscious again, including Jimmy and Bert, who were in police custody, along with Elvira. C.T. was talking with Sergeant Villone.

I walked over to the two of them, holding Sophie's hand. On my way, we passed by the less-than-dynamic duo of Batman and Robin. They were hugging and scream-crying.

"I'm so sorry!" the bogus Batman yelled. "I push people away. I do it with you. With Alfred. With Batgirl. Why? Why do I do that?"

"You're afraid to love, man! But it's okay," Robin said. "I've got enough for both of us."

I joined C.T. as Sergeant Villone walked Jimmy toward a group of officers.

Jimmy yelled at C.T., "I was the Prince of potty humor! You ruined me!"

"You ruined yourself," C.T. said. If you were really any good at potty humor, you would've said I flushed your career down the toilet. I mean, it's not that hard, dude."

As if we needed more chaos in the room, at least six people from the medical crew entered the room to tend to the injured.

A short man and a tall woman came up onto the stage where most of the crazy action was.

The woman looked at C.T.'s bumps and bruises and asked, "Sir, do you need medical attention?"

"Physically?"

"Yes," the woman nodded.

"No. I think I'm okay. Mentally and emotionally? Maybe."

She turned to me and Sophie. "You two look okay. Anything need attention?"

"I'm good," Sophie said.

My pinkie toe hurt, but I couldn't admit that to anyone.

Sergeant Villone walked toward us. I checked for the nearest exits. I wasn't gonna make it. I would just have to take whatever punishment was in store for me. If I had to serve some time, I'd have to serve some time.

I turned to Sophie. "Whatever happens, just know that being your boyfriend has been the greatest experience of my life."

Sophie smiled. "I know." It was very Han Solo-like. I hoped I wouldn't be stuck being Princess Leia for Halloween. I was pretty certain I would not look as good as she would in a white dress with my hair in Cinnabons.

I laughed, as Sergeant Villone cleared his throat. I stood at attention, hoping that nobody could see my knees shaking.

He reached his hands out for mine. I put my wrists out in front of me, the one handcuff swinging in front.

I closed my eyes, unable to watch. My heart was nearly pounding through my chest.

Sergeant Villone said, "I guess I owe you an apology."

I opened one eye, looking to see who he was talking to. He was talking to me!

Sergeant Villone grabbed my cuffed wrist with one hand and his keys with the other. He unlocked the cuffs and slipped them onto his utility belt.

I opened both eyes and exhaled. "That's a pretty cool belt," I said. "It's like Batman's."

Segeant Villone leaned in and said, "Don't tell the Dark Knight I said this, but mine's cooler."

C.T. said, "Not sure about that. You don't have a

batarang." He looked at me and said, "I gotta add that to my Christmas list. Where's Kyle?"

C.T. held out his hand for the sergeant to shake. The sergeant shook it heartily.

"I wish you the best of luck," Sergeant Villone said. "My apologies again."

"It's okay. I will consider upping my Yelp review now that you caught the bad guy and my laptop has been recovered. It's totally useless, but that's not your fault. That's Austin's fault."

"Hey!" I said. "You never would've even known where it was had it not been for us."

"I'm just kidding," he said, smiling. He put his hands on mine and Sophie's shoulders. "Come on. Let's get out of here before something else goes wrong." He nodded to Sergeant Villone. "Any reports of Barking Tree Frogs on the loose?"

The sergeant furrowed his brow. "None that I know of."

"Be on the lookout. They stink and you never know when they may strike."

"Okay," the sergeant said, unsure.

My eyes were drawn to a red suit that entered the room. Well, there was a dude inside it, too. It was the faux Flash from the Garden Inn. The one we asked to watch over the hacker and the henchman, but apparently failed to do so. He walked over to us, gasping for air.

"What happened?" I asked.

"They...escaped," he said.

C.T. asked, "How did they beat you here?" We were both flabbergasted.

The faux Flash shrugged and said, "I didn't eat breakfast?"

C.T. patted him on the shoulder and said, "Well, thanks for trying. You'll get 'em next time."

The Flash nodded with a smile.

"Thanks anyway, I guess," C.T. said.

Faux Flash walked away slowly, his head down.

C.T. looked at me and asked, "Where are your parents, by the way?"

"My dad is on the way," I said.

"Okay. I'll walk you out."

We pushed through the crowds, not really able to talk. I reflected on the day, not sure what to think about it at all. I decided not to think about it. I had one question that I really wanted to ask C.T. when we decided to go to Comic Con.

Once we made it to a quiet area, I looked up at C.T. and asked, "Can I ask you a question?"

"Fire away."

"What's your favorite part about writing?"

"That's easy. I get to create stories from scratch. It's exciting. I can make characters say or do whatever I want. I like to surprise people. You never know when I might kill a character off. Nobody's safe."

I immediately felt nauseous, but didn't know why.

Sophie looked at me. "You okay?"

"Hey, Aus, what's the matter?" C.T. asked.

"Let's talk about something else," I said, holding in my puke.

"Yeah, sure."

We walked outside to the pick-up area. My dad was leaning up against the parked SUV.

"Hey dad!" I waved to him.

"How was the day?"

"Umm, interesting."

He looked at me like parents do when they know you're not telling the whole story. Ben was covering a fat lip with his hand. Sophie had a scratch on her neck that she was hiding with her hair, and Luke quickly slipped on sunglasses to hide a bruise under his eye. I hoped my dad wouldn't notice that my torn jeans were not by a fashion choice, but by a serious kerfuffle.

"What was the most exciting thing that happened?"

I downplayed it. "Waiting on the line to see C.T."

"That exciting, huh?"

My dad looked at C.T. and narrowed his eyes. "You look familiar."

"C.T. Walsh at your service," he said, shaking my dad's hand.

"Nice to meet you."

"Is that blood on your shirt," my dad asked C.T.

"Of course not," he said. "Just ketchup. I had corndog earlier. You should catch one some time."

I held in my chuckle.

C.T. looked at me. "Will I see you here next year? I won't bring my laptop."

"The jury's still out on that one," I said.

"Well, how do I get in touch with you guys if the Fartman project takes off? The studio execs kinda liked it. They said it had explosive potential."

My dad grabbed a business card from his pocket and handed it to C.T. "You can reach me here."

"Sounds good." C.T. looked at me and asked, "Do I owe you anything for bailing me out of jail?"

My dad's face went pale.

C.T. chuckled and said, "Just kidding, sir." He looked at the rest of the crew. "You guys are the most amazing group of friends I've ever come across. Don't ever change. It's been a pleasure." He smiled at us and said, "Now, stay outta trouble, ya hear?"

We all laughed.

"All right," my dad said, with a raised eyebrow. "Hop in the truck. We've got a long drive."

I grabbed the door handle and pulled the door open. Backing up out of the way, I bumped into someone. I turned around, about to apologize, and then my eyes nearly bulged out of my head. It was Voldemort!

"Voldy, what are you doing here? I thought Harry Potter took you out at the pizza place?"

"You dare speak my name?"

"Umm, yeah," I said, as my crew piled into the truck.

The strong-nosed Voldemort reached into his robe and grabbed his wand. "Avada-"

"Ahhhh farts!" I yelled, diving into the back seat of the car.

I closed the door and looked out the window to see C.T. sitting on Voldy's back, his hands beneath his chin, unleashing a devastating Camel Clutch on the Dark Lord.

"That's a weird dude," my dad said.

"If you only knew," I said, laughing.

There were four of us in the middle row, so Ben forced his way between Sophie and me, in an attempt to climb over the seat. In the commotion, a strange barking or honking sound emanated from beneath my seat. It vibrated, too. I hoped everyone would think it was just from Ben's sweaty skin rubbing on the seat, but unfortunately that was not the case.

Sophie turned to me and asked, "What was that?"

Ahhh, farts. Literally. I smiled sheepishly and said, "Barking Tree Frog?"

Got Audio?

Want to listen to Middle School Mayhem?

SCAN ME

ABOUT THE AUTHOR

C.T. Walsh is the author of the Middle School Mayhem Series, set to be a total twelve hilarious adventures of Austin Davenport and his friends.

Besides writing fun, snarky humor and the occasionally-frequent fart joke, C.T. loves spending time with his family, coaching his kids' various sports, and successfully turning seemingly unsandwichable things into spectacular sandwiches, while also claiming that he never eats carbs. He assures you, it's not easy to do. C.T. knows what you're thinking: this guy sounds complex, a little bit mysterious, and maybe even dashingly handsome, if you haven't been to the optometrist in a while. And you might be right.

C.T. finds it weird to write about himself in the third person, so he is going to stop doing that now.

You can learn more about C.T. (oops) at ctwalsh.fun

 facebook.com/ctwalshauthor

ALSO BY C.T. WALSH

Down with the Dance: Book One

Santukkah!: Book Two

The Science (Un)Fair: Book Three

Battle of the Bands: Book Four

Medieval Mayhem: Book Five

The Takedown: Book Six

Valentine's Duh: Book Seven

Future Release schedule

Election Misdirection: June 15th, 2020

Education: Domestication: August 15th, 2020

Class Tripped: September 15th, 2020

Graduation Detonation: November 15th, 2020

Made in the USA
Monee, IL
12 November 2020